"Careful, your libido is showing."

"And I was trying so hard to hide it."

"What's the matter, Josh, no new woman in your life?"

"Not in the usual sense, no."

Bridget's throat had gone very dry. "Then in what sense?"

He needed to leave before he did something stupid. And yet he wasn't moving.

And then he was. But he was moving to close the tiny bit of space between them.

The only way she was going to save herself was through bravado, and she knew it.

"You're in my space, Youngblood," Bridget informed him hoarsely, trying to sound annoyed.

"What are you going to do about it?"

He half expected her to shove him back. The one thing he hadn't expected was for Bridget to grab him and press her mouth urgently against his.

And just before she did, he could have sworn that she'd whispered, "Damn you!"

Dear Reader,

Welcome back to the newest branch of the Cavanaughs, the one belonging to Sean, Brian and Andrew's long-lost brother. This time the story is about Sean's oldest daughter, Bridget, who finds herself grappling with what she views as a brand-new identity. This while becoming aware of feelings for her partner of three years, Josh Youngblood, feelings she has been trying to ignore because, after all, the man's relationships have the life expectancy of a fruit fly.

But Josh surprises her by being the one who is there for her while she's trying to sort out how she feels about this new family connection that has suddenly cropped up in her life as well as the lives of her immediate family members. And all this is played out while Bridget and Josh desperately try to bring down The Lady Killer, a serial killer who surfaces every February to kill as many redheaded women between the ages of twenty and thirty as he can in that short month. Interested? Then please keep reading. I promise to try to entertain you as best as I can.

With all my heart I wish you someone to love who loves you back.

Until the next time,

Marie Ferrarella

MARIE FERRARELLA

Cavanaugh's Bodyguard

ROMANTIC
SUSPENSE

Recycling programs
for this product may
not exist in your area.

ISBN-13: 978-0-373-27769-8

CAVANAUGH'S BODYGUARD

Books by Marie Ferrarella

Harlequin Romantic Suspense

Silhouette Romantic Suspense

Harlequin Special Edition

Silhouette Special Edition

American Romance

Other titles by this author available in ebook format.

MARIE FERRARELLA

This *USA TODAY* bestselling and RITA® Award-winning author has written more than two hundred books for Harlequin Books and Silhouette Books, some under the name Marie Nicole. Her romances are beloved by fans worldwide. Visit her website at www.marieferrarella.com.

To Charlie,
who turned the month of February
into something special
all those years ago.

Chapter 1

Finally.

The thought flashed through Detective Bridget Cavelli's mind at the same time that she glanced up to verify that the movement she'd detected out of the corner of her eye was her partner and no one else. She'd been waiting for her sexier-than-should-be-legally-allowed partner, Detective Joshua Youngblood, to walk into the squad room for the last half hour. This was precisely the amount of time she'd been going over the notes she had taken a year ago this month.

Her partner wasn't late. He was on time. She was the one who was early, but that didn't help to assuage her impatience. She needed to share this with him.

Now.

She struggled to rein in her impatience. It could have been worse. He could have been coming off a forty-eight-hour marathon date and running late rather than coming in right on time.

"He's back," Bridget announced to her partner, raising her voice in order to catch his attention.

Detective Joshua Youngblood said nothing in response as he continued walking to his desk. His green eyes were hidden behind exceptionally dark sunglasses. His measured, rhythmic gait brought him to the desk that had been assigned to him for the last three years.

After setting down the extra large container of ink-black coffee, Josh set himself down as well. His chair groaned. It needed oiling.

Once he was seated opposite her did he even acknowledge that he'd heard what Bridget had said by asking in a monotone voice, "Who's back?"

Bridget, who'd been his partner for as long as he'd been at this desk, leaned back slightly in her chair as she studied his expressionless face. The fact that Josh was still partially hidden behind the sunglasses told her all she needed to know. It was Monday and more likely than not, Josh hadn't amassed enough sleep over the weekend to keep a squirrel bright-eyed and bushy-tailed or even moderately functioning.

Temporarily forgetting the very cold chill that had gone zigzagging down her spine when the new acting lieutenant had told her the news earlier, Bridget asked her zombie-channeling partner a personal question, taking care not to show the slight spike of jealousy she suddenly experienced. "So, what's this one's name?"

For the time being, Josh left his sunglasses on. "I have no idea what you're talking about."

He was focused on removing the lid from the newly purchased, life-affirming black liquid. Josh absolutely *hated* tasting plastic when he drank his coffee and no matter how careful he tried to be, if he left the lid on, he could taste plastic with each sip.

This morning his hands felt like clumsy bear paws. This was what he got for going to bed ninety minutes before he was due in to work, he silently upbraided himself.

With a suppressed sigh, Bridget rose from her desk and made her way around to his. With a flick of her wrist, she made quick work of the coffee lid, tossing it into his waste paper basket. A thin plume of steam rose up from the inky sea.

"So, this one evaporated your brain as well as your energy?" she asked glibly, deliberately sounding chipper as she commented, "Busy little bee."

"I was up with a sick friend," Josh informed her after he had taken an incredibly long sip of his coffee. He could feel it winding through his system. Ever so slowly, he began to feel human again.

"I've never known you to make a woman sick, Josh. A little nauseous maybe, but not sick." Leaning her hip against his desk, Bridget crossed her arms before her and shook her head as she pinned him with a penetrating look. "Don't you think you should start acting your age, Youngblood? Partying and staying out all night all weekend is great when you're in college or in your early twenties, but all that's supposed to be out of your system by the time you start approaching thirty."

Josh appeared not to be paying any attention to her. Then he surprised her by sighing. "If you're going to lecture me—" he began.

She pretended to hang on his every word. "Yes?"

He took in a huge fortifying breath before warning her, "Don't."

A thousand little devils with tiny hammers pounded and danced around in his head. He was in no mood to listen to a lecture or any so-called words of wisdom his overly talkative partner might want to impart. From the first moment he'd seen her, he'd been of the opinion that she was exceptionally easy on the eyes, but definitely not always so easy on the ears.

"I'm just trying to look out for you, Partner," Bridget told him, deliberately smiling brightly at him. "Because whatever you do reflects on me." With that, she removed the black sunglasses from his face and gingerly placed them on his desk next to his computer. She did a quick assessment of his face. The last three days had left their mark. She couldn't remember ever seeing him this exhausted, and that included the time they had pulled a double surveillance shift.

Bridget told herself that it shouldn't bother her that he spent all his free time with women whose bust sizes were higher than their IQs—but it did.

Just sisterly concern, nothing more, she silently insisted.

"I suppose you don't look so bad—for a hungover Peter Pan," she commented.

"I'm not hungover," Josh protested, although without much verve. "For your information, I had the flu this weekend and I'm trying to get over it."

She raised a skeptical eyebrow. That hadn't taken long. She'd caught him in a lie already. "I thought you said you were up with a sick friend."

Josh never hesitated or wavered. "Where do you think I got the flu?"

He sounded almost indignant, but she wasn't buying it, not for a second. She knew him too well. Joshua Youngblood, second-generation cop and handsomer than sin, was a consummate ladies' man from the word *go.* The verb was also his rule of thumb whenever things began to look even remotely serious. The second a woman stopped viewing him less as a good time and more as husband material, Josh was gone. To his credit, he made no secret of it, made no promises that took in a month from now, much less "forever."

"You know," Bridget said glibly, "you might think about becoming a writer. I hear a lot of cops with a gift for fantasy start spinning stories on paper in their free time. Who knows? You might find your name on the binding of a book someday."

A third big gulp came precariously close to draining his container despite its large size. Josh set the cup down and did his best to focus his attention on Bridget. The woman was smart as well as a damn good detective. There was no one who he would rather have watching his back than her, but at times he could easily strangle her as well.

Like now.

All he wanted was to have his coffee in peace and then slowly ease into his day. Hopefully accomplishing both with a minimum of noise and pain until he could focus not just his mind but his eyes.

Didn't look as if that would happen. What he needed to do since he couldn't strangle her—at least not in a building full of cops—was deflect Bridget's attention away from him.

"You said something about someone being back," he reminded her. The coffee, strong enough to be used as a substitute for asphalt in a pinch, was beginning to finally work its magic. All he needed was another half hour or so before last night, Ivy Potter and the now empty bottle of Southern Comfort were all securely behind him.

"Yes, I did."

He sighed. Obviously she was going to make him work for this. "Okay, who's back?" he repeated.

"Who do you think?" Bridget crossed back to her desk and, for the moment, sat down. Or rather, she perched on the edge of her chair, too much tension dancing through her body for her to sit down properly.

"If I knew, I wouldn't be asking, would I?" Josh retorted with more than a trace of irritability in his voice.

As he spoke, he began to go through his drawers, opening one after another and rifling through them. He was searching for a bottle of desperately needed aspirin. If he didn't find it soon, he was damn near certain that the top of his head would come off.

Instead of answering him, Bridget asked, "What month is it?"

Frustrated, Josh raised his eyes to hers for a moment. "More tough questions?" he quipped. When she didn't say anything, he sighed, clearly exasperated as he continued with his up to this point fruitless search.

Damn it, there'd been a huge bottle of aspirin here just the other day. It couldn't have just disappeared. *Where* is *it?* he silently demanded.

"February," Josh bit off. "What does that have to do with—" And then he stopped and raised his eyes to hers again. The answer came crashing back to him. He fervently hoped he was wrong. *Very* fervently. "February," he repeated.

"February," Bridget echoed grimly with a nod of her head.

On her feet again, she went back to his desk. Moving him out of the way, she opened the bottom drawer, which was deeper than the rest, and, reaching in, she pushed aside several folders. Extracting the white and green bottle she knew he was looking for, she placed it on Josh's blotter in front of him without a word. She didn't need to talk. Her meaning was clear. Even though he was a great detective, there were times when the man had trouble finding his face when he was looking into the mirror.

What went unsaid, and she would have gone to her grave denying it, was that the trait was somewhat endearing to her.

Grabbing the bottle the second she'd produced it for him, Josh twisted off the top, shook out two rectangular pills and popped them into his mouth. He downed them with the last few drops of coffee lingering on the bottom of the giant container. Now all he could do was wait for the aspirin to take effect.

With a deep breath, he leaned back in his chair and fixed his partner with an incredulous look. "I was really hoping he was dead."

Bridget nodded. "Weren't we all," she readily agreed.

"You sure it was him?" Josh asked grimly. Before her eyes, he seemed to transform from the exceptionally handsome playboy who thought a long-term relationship meant one that lasted from one weekend to the next, into the razor-sharp investigator with keen instincts she both enjoyed and looked forward to working with.

Bridget answered him by reciting the details she'd

just read of the latest victim's description. "Pretty red-head in her early twenties. Her hands were neatly folded just above her abdomen and she had a big, gaping hole in her chest where her heart used to be. Yeah, I'm sure."

She sighed, shaking her head as she picked up the folder the lieutenant had given her and brought it over to Josh for his examination. After his last spree, the serial killer, whimsically dubbed the Lady Killer by a label-hungry media, had disappeared for almost a year and they had all nursed the hope that this time it was because he was dead and not because he seemed to have a quirk about the month when Cupid was celebrated.

"You know, I'm really beginning to hate Februar-ies," she told him.

Preoccupied with scanning the report submitted by the initial officer on the scene, Josh read that the po-liceman had found the body laid out in an alley behind a popular night club. Belatedly, Bridget's words regis-tered in his head.

He glanced up and spared her an amused, know-ing look. "I bet you were the little girl in elementary school who always got the most valentines dropped off at her desk on Valentine's Day." Bridget was the kind of woman the label "hot" had been coined for and there were times that he had to stop and remind himself that she was his partner and that he couldn't cross the lines that he ordinarily stepped over without a second thought. There would be consequences and he liked working with her too much to risk them.

"Then you would have lost that bet," Bridget told him matter-of-factly. "I was the girl in elementary school who never got any." She could vividly remem-ber hating the approach of the holiday each year, her feelings of inadequacy ballooning to giant proportions every February fourteenth.

Josh looked up from the folder, surprised. "None?" he questioned suspiciously.

Bridget had to be pulling his leg for some strange reason of her own. Blond, with incredibly vivid blue eyes and a killer figure that not even a burlap sack could disguise, she had to have legions of guys drooling over her since she had first emerged out of her crib.

And, he thought again, he would have been among them if fate hadn't made them partners in the field.

"None," Bridget confirmed with a sharp nod of her head. It was still painful to recall those days and the way she'd felt. There were times now, when she looked into the mirror, that she felt as if that insecure little girl were still alive and well inside her. "I was a real ugly duckling as a kid," she told him. "I absolutely hated Valentine's Day back then. It always made me feel awkward, like everyone was looking at me and knew that I didn't get a single card from anyone. I thought it was a horrible holiday."

"Maybe that's it," Josh said, closing the sparse report and watching her.

Bridget looked at him, curious. She'd obviously missed something. "What's 'it'?"

"Maybe the killer is some psycho getting even," he suggested. As he spoke, it began to make more and more sense to him. "Our guy asked this redheaded goddess out on a date for Valentine's Day and she turned him down, maybe even laughed at him for daring to ask her." As he spoke, Josh's voice grew louder and more resonant. "His pride wounded, he doesn't step aside and lick his wounds like most guys, he gets even. *Really* gets even.

"Now, every February, he's relives that—or maybe relives what he wanted to do but didn't at the time—and takes out his revenge on girls who look like the one who rejected him."

Bridget turned what Josh had just said over in her head, studying it. "So what are you telling me? That you think our killer is Charlie Brown?" she asked him, amused despite the gruesome details of the case.

It seemed almost absurd—except for the fact that it did keep on happening. In the last two years, nine red-heads, their hearts very neatly cut out, had been found in alleys throughout Aurora.

Josh surprised her by explaining why her tongue-in-cheek theory didn't hold. "No, Charlie Brown never got his nerve up to ask the little redheaded girl out, so she couldn't reject him. She's just his eternal dream."

His eternal dream. That was almost poetic, she thought.

Bridget eyed her partner, amazed—and amused. Every time that she was about to write him off as being shallow, there'd be this glimmer of sensitivity that would just pull her back in.

She supposed that was one of the reasons women always flocked to him. That, a small waist and a rock-solid body that showed off his active gym membership.

"My God, Youngblood, I'm impressed," she told him after a beat. "I had no idea that you were so sensitive."

Josh stared at her for a long moment. And then his smile, the one she'd dubbed his "bad boy" smile, which could melt the heart of a statue, curved the corners of his mouth. "There're lot of things about me that you don't know."

Now he was just trying to jockey for leverage and mess with her mind, Bridget thought. There was just one little flaw with his allegation.

"I grew up with four brothers." She loved all of them dearly, but at times, when she'd been growing up, the verbal fights had been brutal. "They'd more than held their own, but I really doubt that there's very much about a living, breathing male that I can't second-guess," she told Josh with a smile.

Before Josh could say anything in response, their acting lieutenant, Jack Howard, came out of his office, saw them and immediately came over. Howard, a rather self-centered man who enjoyed hearing the sound of his own voice, had been the one to hand Bridget the case this morning once he saw that she and Youngblood had worked on it a year ago.

He looked from Bridget to Josh. "You two solve the case yet?" he asked in what appeared to be genuine seriousness.

Bridget knew better than to think he was kidding when he asked the question, but she played along, uncertain where this *was* going. She had a gut feeling that wherever it was, neither she nor Josh were going to like it. There was something very pompous about the man. Added to that, she had a feeling that he resented the fact that she was related to the police department's well-respected hierarchy.

"No, sir, not yet," she answered, allowing her voice to be neither submissive nor combative. She merely gave him the respect that his position was due. It had nothing to do with the man.

She and Josh had originally heard about the case two years ago, after the second body had been discovered. None of the clues at the time had led the investigating detectives anywhere substantial. Four bodies had turned up and then the killer seemed to just vanish into thin air.

Until last February when he surfaced again.

This time, the case became theirs and the killer wound up leaving five women in his wake, five women who were all left in the same pose as this latest one. Hands neatly folded below where their hearts should have been. All in all, it made for a very gruesome picture.

"Then why are you just sitting around?" Howard demanded, his voice no longer friendly. He turned on Bridget. "Just because you suddenly found out that your uncle's the chief of detectives doesn't give you any extra points in my book or cut you any extra slack. Do you understand Cavelli—Cavanaugh?" Flummoxed, he glared at her. "What the hell do you want me to call you?" Howard demanded.

Bridget squared her shoulders like a soldier who had found herself under fire and was making the best of it. She didn't like Howard, and his harping on her recent situation just underscored her negative feelings for the man.

God, would this tempest in a teapot never be resolved? It was bad enough that Josh had teased her about it. But he at least didn't seem jealous of this brand-new status she found herself struggling with, a status she'd never sought out or wanted in the first place.

But here it was, anyway.

Ever since the five-decades-old mix-up in the hospital had come to light, uncovering the fact that her father and some other infant male had accidentally been switched at birth and that her father—and so, consequently affecting all the rest of them—was not Sean Cavelli but Sean Cavanaugh, brother to both the former police chief and the current chief of detectives of the Aurora Police Department, she and her siblings had had no peace.

They were assaulted with questions, innuendos and their share of jealous remarks on a regular basis. They were no longer judged on their own merits but on the fact that they were all part of what was considered by others to be the "royal family" of the police department.

Now that she actually thought about it, it seemed as if there was at least one Cavanaugh in almost every branch of the department. Despite the fact that it was completely without a basis, nepotism and favoritism were words that were constantly being bandied about when it came to talk about their jobs and she for one was sick of it.

She'd gotten here by her own merit long before she'd ever been made aware of her surprising connection to the Cavanaughs.

It was enough to make a woman bitter, Bridget thought, eternally grateful that she at least had a large, thriving optimistic streak coupled with healthy dose of self-esteem—now.

"'Detective' will do fine," Bridget informed the lieutenant with a deliberate, wide smile that might have been called flirtatious under somewhat different circumstances.

Josh wasn't fooled. He knew she'd flashed the smile

on purpose, to throw Howard off and confuse him. If he didn't miss his guess, his partner would have rather eaten dirt than be even remotely coupled with the new lieutenant and the fact that Howard was married had nothing to do with it. He'd only been on the job for a day before it became apparent that Jack Howard had an ego the size of Pittsburgh.

"Well, 'Detective,'" the lieutenant said curtly, giving her a withering glance, "you and your sleepy-looking partner can get off your butts and do some honest police work and catch this son of a bitch before he louses up my record for cleared cases!" Howard snapped.

With that, the lieutenant turned on the heel of his Italian leather, three-hundred-dollar shoes, and marched back into his office, confident that he had made a dramatic impact on not just the two detectives but the rest of the squad room as well.

Josh glanced over toward Bridget and saw the way her hand closed over the stapler on her desk—like she was debating hurling it.

He put his hand over hers, keeping the stapler where it was. "Not worth it, partner," he murmured.

She took a deep breath and nodded, doing her best to ignore the momentary warm feeling that zipped through her and then vanished the second Josh removed his hand from hers.

Chapter 2

"*His* record," Bridget bit off angrily, struggling not to raise her voice loud enough for the retreating lieutenant to hear her. "That jerk couldn't clear a case if it was lying on the floor and he had a broom in his hands. We're the ones who clear cases," she declared hotly, referring not just to herself and Josh, but to the other detectives who were in their division as well. They were the ones who did all the work, not Howard. He turned up at the press conferences to grab the recognition, but he was never there for the hard work.

"Don't work yourself up," Josh advised mildly. "Like I said, it's not worth it. And, while you're at it," he continued, leaning in so that his voice was even lower than it was a moment ago, "don't raise your voice."

She glared at Josh. How could he remain so calm

around that preening peacock? "It isn't raised," she insisted.

"No," he agreed. Her eyes narrowed into blue slits of suppressed fire that he found arousing. "But it will be," he pointed out. "And this headache is still killing me."

Bridget looked over her shoulder toward Howard's office and at the man inside the glass enclosure. He was watching them. It just made her temper rise to a dangerous level.

"Speaking of killing…"

On his feet, Josh came up behind his partner and placed both hands on her back. With a gentle push, he guided her toward the doorway. "Let's go, Cavelli, before I suddenly find myself having to break in a brand-new partner. You know how much I'd hate that."

Forcing herself to calm down, Bridget spared Josh an amused glance as she doubled back to get her jacket. He really did look out for her, and she appreciated it. He was a hell of a lot more thoughtful than some of the guys she'd dated.

Too bad circumstances weren't different, she mused as she deposited something into her pocket before slipping on her light gray jacket.

"Breaking in a new partner," she echoed. "Who are you kidding?" she asked. "Nobody would be able to put up with you and your quirks for more than a week."

"And I'd find myself missing that unabashed, everflowing flattery of yours," Josh cracked as he led the way to the elevator. "By the way…" He turned toward her. "Exactly where are we supposed to be going?"

She'd stuffed the details of this year's first murder into her jacket and pulled it out now as they waited for the elevator to arrive. Pointing to the pertinent addresses, she held the sheet up for her partner to see.

"We can either go to the scene of the crime or go to break the news to the victim's boyfriend. Take your pick." Folding the sheets again, she slipped them back into her pocket. "I'm guessing that the ME hasn't had a chance to do the autopsy yet, otherwise, *that* would be my first pick."

Josh made his choice. As he saw it, it was the lesser of two evils. "Scene of the crime," he said as they stepped into the elevator. After a beat, he made a confession, which was rare for him. "I absolutely hate breaking that kind of news to people. They're never the same after that."

Bridget laughed shortly. "Haven't found anyone yet who *didn't* mind it, never mind enjoyed it." She clearly remembered each time she'd had to go to a loved one to break the tragic news. The experience never became routine. Her heart hurt every time. "Okay, scene of the crime it is." She leaned forward and pressed for the ground floor. "You realize that putting it off doesn't make telling the boyfriend any easier."

He knew that, but he was hoping for another option. "And nobody else caught this case?" he asked just before the doors opened again on the ground floor.

Bridget made an elaborate show of searching the small aluminum-walled enclosure. "You see anyone else here?"

"Nope," he answered, resigning himself to the fact that they were working the gruesome case solo as they got off. "But that's only because you're so dynamic you make everyone else fade into the background."

Bridget stopped just short of the rear doors that

exited out onto the parking lot. Turning, she looked at Josh quizzically. "What's with you this morning?" she asked.

Wide shoulders rose and fell in a noncommittal shrug. Since she wasn't going through the doors, he did. And then he held them open for her.

"Nothing," he responded dismissively.

Bridget slipped through the doors quickly. She wasn't about to give up that easily.

"Yes, there is," she insisted. They were on the same wavelength, she and Josh. Something was off. She could feel her protective side being roused. "Now spill it. Your latest main squeeze hounding you for a commitment?" she guessed, deliberately keeping her voice upbeat and light. The idea of her partner committing to a single woman was as far-fetched as Prince Charming actually turning out to be a skilled day laborer. And, if she were being utterly honest with herself, she rather liked it that way.

Why should that matter? she silently upbraided herself. *The guy's your partner, not your lover, remember?*

It annoyed her that the word "lover" had even popped into her head in reference to Josh. What was with her lately?

Josh paused, gazing out on the parking lot. He wasn't looking for his car—he knew where that was—he was looking for his patience, which seemed to be in short supply this morning.

"No, not her," he finally said.

Bridget heard things in his voice that he was leaving unsaid.

Not for long, she thought.

"Then who is?" she asked. Josh merely frowned in

response and went down the cement steps, heading toward the vehicle they were using for the day. Bridget followed quickly.

But, getting into the passenger seat, she paused for a second and offered to switch places with him. Whether hungover, coming down with something or disturbed, he wasn't himself today.

"You want me to drive?" she asked.

"Nope." Josh buckled up. "I'm not ready to die today," he told her.

Bridget was quiet for a moment, trying to get to the bottom of what was eating at him. And then it hit her. Belatedly, she finally buckled up.

"It's your mother, isn't it?" she guessed just as he turned the key in the ignition. The car came to life and he slowly backed out of his space.

"It's my mother what?" he asked shortly, straightening out the wheel and then heading out onto the main thoroughfare.

She ignored the shortness of Josh's response. "It's your mother who's hounding you to make a commitment, isn't it?"

Damn it, he thought irritably, the woman was like a pit bull once she latched onto something. She just wouldn't let go. "Not sure how things are done in your world, Cavelli, but in this state, mothers and sons can't get married."

She was right, Bridget thought. She could tell by the set of his jaw. "You know damn well what I'm saying, Youngblood." This wasn't the first time his mother, a really affable woman, had been on his case. "Your mother's after you to settle down, isn't she?"

He gave up trying to get her to back off. "Grandkids," he declared, annoyed. He really loved his mother. They had gotten extremely close after his father had been killed in the line of duty and as far as mothers went, she was rather sharp and with it—except for this one annoying flaw. "She says she wants grandkids. I told her she was too young for that."

"Flattery." She nodded her approval. "Nice. Did it work?"

He laughed shortly and shook his head. "Nope. She says there're a lot of young grandmothers around these days. According to her, she's the only one of her friends whose kid is still single."

"She's lonely," Bridget guessed, feeling for the woman. She'd met Eva Youngblood a number of times and found her to be extremely affable. They got along really well. The woman would make someone a really nice mother-in-law someday. "That's what you get for being an only child."

"Hey, it's not my fault," Josh pointed out. "After my dad died, lots of his buddies on the force came around to make sure we were all right. They took turns bringing me to ball games, coaching my team, helping me study. They did what they could to be there for her, too. I know that more than one of them really wanted to get serious with her."

He frowned, remembering what it was like, hearing his mother cry late at night when she thought he was asleep. It broke his heart and made him promise to himself that he would never love someone so much that he couldn't breathe right without them.

"But Mom swore up and down that Dad had been the love of her life and she was not looking to get married again. Ever. And even if she was, it wouldn't be to another policeman. She said she couldn't go through that kind of pain again. Couldn't stand there and be on the receiving end of a condolence call."

Bridget supposed she could understand that. Once hurt, twice leery. "So, instead of building a second life," she surmised, "your mother is after you to finally build yours."

He sighed. "That's about it."

Parents, she knew, could be exceedingly stubborn when it came to their kids. Her father was laid-back, thank God, but her late mother had been fairly intense. Looking back, she realized it was all out of love, but at the time it had driven her crazy.

"So, what are you going to do?" Bridget asked, slanting a glance in his direction.

He'd already looked into this solution. "I'm going to get her a dog."

Bridget laughed, pretending to study his profile for a moment. "I can see the resemblance, but I really don't think that's what your mother actually has in mind."

Whether she did or not, this was the plan for now. He was stalling for time until something better occurred to him. "I'll tell her it's just a placeholder until I find the girl of my dreams."

Surprised, Bridget shifted in her seat. This was a side of Josh she hadn't expected. In the three years they'd been partnered, Josh had only gotten serious about their work, not about any of the myriad women he'd gone out with in that time.

She caught herself holding her breath as she asked, "You actually have a dream girl?"

"Yeah." Josh spared her a quick, meaningful look.

"One who doesn't ask me any questions or make any demands of me."

For a minute there, she'd thought he was serious. She should have known better. Bridget laughed, shaking her head. Feeling relieved more than she thought she should. "Then I'm afraid that you're doomed to being alone, Youngblood."

"I'm not going to be alone," he told her. They came to a stop at a light. He took the opportunity to turn toward her and flashed a wide, brilliant grin. "I have you."

The very first time she'd seen that smile, it had gotten to her. She hadn't grown immune to its effects, but at this point she knew that he meant nothing by it. He was just charming. And while she caught herself wondering what it would be like to be with Josh, *really* be with Josh, who could have been the living, breathing poster child for the words "drop dead gorgeous," she told herself that she didn't want to ruin a good thing. She and Josh worked well together, anticipated one another and for the most part, thought alike.

At times they wound up completing one another; what one lacked, the other supplied. Partnerships like that were exceedingly rare, not worth sacrificing in order to scratch an itch.

She'd been quiet too long, she realized. To deflect any kind of suspicions or possible questions on Josh's end, she got back to the reason they were out here in the first place. "Yeah, well, if we don't come up with some kind of answers for the narcissistic fool they made our acting lieutenant, Howard might wind up splitting us up out of spite."

He sincerely doubted that would ever happen. When

they had first been paired, all he saw was what one of his late father's friends had described as a "hot babe." It didn't take Bridget very long to set him straight. She might have killer looks, but it was her brain power that he actually found sexy. The fact that she didn't trade on her looks was another plus in her favor.

It also allowed him the freedom to tease her now. "You could always go and complain about Howard to your 'Uncle Brian.'"

Bridget sat up a little straighter as she gave him a withering look. "Hello, possibly we haven't been introduced yet. My name's Bridget Cavelli and I fight my own battles."

"So, you're keeping it?" Josh asked, picking up on the name she'd used. "You're not changing it?"

"Changing what?"

"Your last name. Technically, you are a Cavanaugh, you know. You have no real ties to that moniker you've been sporting around for the last thirty years—"

"Twenty-eight," she corrected tersely. "I'm twenty-eight."

He knew exactly how old she was—knew a great many other things about her as well—but he liked getting under her skin. It helped to keep things light. It also helped him deflect other feelings he was having. Feelings that had no place on the job and would only get in the way of a working relationship.

"And you don't look a day over twenty-seven and a half," he deadpanned.

Bridget sighed and settled back in her seat. It was going to be a very long morning, she thought. She could tell.

* * *

"Andrew, are you all right? You look a little pale," Rose Cavanaugh said to her husband, stopping short.

She'd just walked into the state-of-the-art kitchen to get a glass of juice. This was where the former chief of police and the love of her life spent a great deal of his time each day. He could be found here creating or re-creating meals for any one of a vast number of relatives who had a standing invitation to drop by whenever the occasion allowed, or they were in the neighborhood. She'd never known anyone who loved cooking—and family—as much as Andrew did.

But it was obvious that right now, he had more on his mind than cooking. Like the person he'd just finished talking to.

"Who was on the phone?" she asked him as Andrew hung up the receiver.

He tried to offer his wife a smile, but he was still sorting out the news he'd just received. "That was my father."

The family patriarch, Seamus Cavanaugh, was the first of the family to join the police department and work his way through the ranks, back when Aurora was unincorporated and considered an off-shoot of Sacramento. For the last dozen years or so the retired police chief had been living in Miami Beach, Florida, enjoying the company of some of his old friends from the force who had also migrated there.

Rose smiled fondly. Her father-in-law liked to check in from time to time. He did it in order to keep his sons from worrying, although he insisted that he was perfectly capable of looking after himself.

"What's he up to?" she asked, wondering what had prompted this particular call. If she knew Seamus, the man was probably in love—again—and asking Andrew what he thought about getting a new "mother."

"About thirty thousand feet," Andrew answered matter-of-factly.

Rose cocked her head, trying to make sense out of what her husband was saying. "Come again?"

"He is," Andrew confirmed. "Coming back again." After taking a fresh cup from the cabinet next to the sink, Andrew poured himself some of the coffee he'd just brewed right before the phone had rung. Holding the cup in both hands, he sat down before he attempted to clarify his statement. "Dad's flying back to Aurora right now, even as we're having this conversation."

Sitting down opposite him, Rose placed her hand on top of her husband's in a mute display of unity.

"Is something wrong?" she asked, concerned. They had been trying to get Seamus to come back out for a visit for years now. But he had always been very adamant about not flying. Because of that, the senior Cavanaugh had missed out on a host of weddings and births.

He'd even passed on what Andrew felt had been a major event in his life: finding Rose again after his wife had gone missing and had been presumed by everyone—everyone but him—to be dead. He never gave up working the case, never gave up looking for the mother of his five children. And eventually, his persistence had paid off. The only thing that remotely came close to spoiling the event for him was that his father had sent his hearty congratulations instead of turning up to celebrate with the rest of the family.

"No, nothing's wrong," Andrew told her. "He said he suddenly just got tired of doing nothing with the rest of his life but shooting the breeze with a bunch of old men who were living in the past. He's decided to turn over a new leaf. Part of that involves flying out here. And, I suspect that he's anxious to meet his new son."

Rose smiled. "At his age, Sean can't exactly be called 'new,'" she pointed out, amusement curving the generous corners of her mouth.

He looked at it in another way. "Considering the fact that Dad's never seen him, I think the word 'new' could be applied in this case."

"I suppose you're right." Pushing aside the empty juice glass, Rose got to her feet. "Well, I'd better get myself to the store," she announced. She caught her husband arching his eyebrow in a silent query, which surprised her. "If there's going to be another one of Andrew Cavanaugh's famous parties in the very near future, I've got a lot of grocery shopping to do. Do you have a list ready for me?"

Instead of producing one, Andrew caught her hand and pulled her over to him, stopping his wife from leaving the room.

"No, no list and no famous party," he told her. "I think that this time around, Dad meeting his son for the first time will be a private occasion."

He could have knocked her over with a feather. "Really?" she asked incredulously.

In all the years that she had been part of Andrew's life, she'd found that absolutely *everything* was an excuse for a family get-together and a party. "One for all and all for one" wasn't just a famous phrase written by Alexander Dumas in *The Three Musketeers*, it was a mantra that she strongly suspected her husband believed in and lived by.

"Dad's got a pretty tight rein on his emotions,"

Andrew explained. Friendly and seemingly outgoing, there was still a part of Seamus Cavanaugh that he kept walled in, strictly to himself. That part grieved over loss and mourned over victims who couldn't be saved in time. "But this kind of thing can just blow a man right out of the water. If, once he meets Sean, Dad loses it, he definitely won't appreciate it happening in front of a room full of witnesses."

Rose laughed. "Since when have we *ever* been able to fit all our relatives into just a room?" she asked.

"All right, I stand corrected. A house full of witnesses," Andrew amended. "This is definitely one case of the less people being around for the grand reunion, the better."

Rose pretended to be disappointed—but the hint of a grin gave her away. "And here I was, planning to sell tickets."

"C'mere, woman." Andrew laughed.

He gave her hand a quick tug and swept her onto his lap. He liked having her there just fine. In his mind, because he'd been given a second chance after doggedly searching for her all those years she'd had amnesia and been missing without realizing it, he still felt like a newlywed.

"Anyone ever tell you that you have a fresh mouth?" he asked Rose, doing his best to sound serious.

Rose laced her fingers together behind his neck as she made herself comfortable in her favorite "chair." "Not that I recall," she answered with a straight face. "Why? Do you want to sample it?"

The former chief of police grinned and looked every bit the boy whom she had first fallen in love with in second-period American English all those very many years ago.

"I thought you'd never ask," he said just before he kissed her and rocked her world.

Again.

Chapter 3

The good-looking man behind the bar whose biceps were more impressive than his brain cells frowned as he stared at the photograph Josh had placed on the counter in front of him. It was a photograph of the woman who had been found in the alley behind the club where he worked and even though the more gruesome aspects of the murder weren't detailed, it was obvious that the woman was dead.

Shaking his head, the bartender, who claimed his name was Simon Quest, looked up at the two detectives.

"I'm a lot better with regulars," he protested. "But yeah, I think she was here last night."

My kingdom for a witness who actually witnessed something, Josh thought. The bartender sounded far from convincing. For now, he left the photograph on the bar, hoping that it still might jog Quest's memory.

"Was anyone bothering her?" Josh asked the other man.

Quest shrugged, as if to dismiss the question, but then he stopped abruptly and pulled the photo over to study it.

Josh's hope sank when he shook his head. "Not that I can recall. It was a happy crowd last night."

Bridget glanced at the victim's pale face. "I know at least one of them who didn't stay that way," she commented grimly.

"Can you remember anything at all about this woman?" Josh prodded Quest one last time. "Was she the life of the party? Was she in a corner, drinking by herself? Anything at all?" he stressed.

The bartender thought for a long moment; then his expression brightened. "I saw her talking to the people around her. They acted as if they all knew each other." Pausing, he appeared as if he was trying to remember something.

When the silence went on too long, Bridget urged the man on. "What?"

"There was this one guy," Simon responded slowly, as if he was envisioning the scene again. "He just kept staring at her."

"Did he come up and talk to her?" Bridget asked eagerly.

Quest shook his head helplessly. "Not that I saw. It was big crowd," he explained, then added, "and we were shorthanded last night."

"What else can you remember about this guy?"

Josh asked, hoping they could finally get something to go on.

"Nothing." The bartender went back to drying the shot glasses that were all lined up in front of him like tiny, transparent soldiers. "He left."

Maybe they could get a time frame, Bridget thought. "When?"

Quest set down another glass, then shrugged again. "I dunno. Around midnight. Maybe one o'clock. I remember she was gone when we closed down," he volunteered, then ruined it by adding, "Can't say when, though."

This was getting them nowhere, Bridget thought. "Did she leave with anyone?"

The look on Quest's face said he had no idea if the victim did or not. He lifted his wide shoulders and then let them drop again. "She was just gone."

Ever hopeful, Bridget tried another approach. "This guy, the one who was staring at her, what did he look like?"

Quest exhaled a frustrated breath. It was obvious that he was regretting he'd ever mentioned the starer. "Just an average guy. Looked like he hadn't cracked a smile in a real long time."

Josh tried his hand at getting some kind of useful information out of the vacant-headed bartender. "Was he young, old, fat, skinny, long-haired, bald, white, black—polka dot," he finally bit off in exasperation when the bartender made no indication that *anything* was ringing a bell.

"Just average," Quest repeated. "Maybe he was forty, maybe not. He did have hair," he recalled. "Kinda messy, like he was trying to look cool but he didn't know how. And he was a white guy. He *wasn't* a regular," Simon emphasized proudly. "Or I would've recognized him."

Well, he supposed at least it was *something*, Josh told himself. He took out one of his cards and placed it on the counter, even as he collected the photograph and tucked it back into his inside pocket.

"You think of anything else you forgot to mention, anything comes back to you—" he tapped the card with his finger "—call me."

Quest shifted his glance toward Bridget. "I'd rather call her."

Information was information, Bridget reasoned. Inclining her head in silent assent, she placed her card next to Josh's on the shiny bar.

"Fine. Here's my card. Just remember," she informed the man cheerfully as she stepped back, "we're a set."

"He was trying to hit on you," Josh told her as they walked out of the club three minutes later. The fact that it bothered him was only because he was being protective of his partner. Or so he told himself. Bridget seemed unaware that she had this aura of sexuality about her and it was up to him to make sure no one tried to take advantage of that.

Right, like she can't take care of herself, Josh silently mocked himself.

He blew out a breath. Maybe he needed more aspirins to clear his head a little better.

Bridget headed straight for the car. "He's lucky I didn't hit him back," she retorted, then complained, "I thought bartenders were supposed to have such great memories."

"Sometimes they're paid not to have them," Josh

speculated, aiming his remote at the car. It squawked in response as four side locks sprang up at attention.

Bridget paused beside the vehicle. "You think he knows more than he's saying?"

Josh laughed shortly. He looked at her over the car's roof. "It would be hard for him to know less. Let's talk to her boyfriend and find out if he knows who she was partying with last night."

She nodded. "Maybe one of them remembers something about this guy who was staring at her."

Getting into the front passenger seat, Bridget buckled up and then let out a loud sigh. After Josh pulled out of the area and back onto the road again, she turned toward him and asked, "So, what kind of a dog?" When he didn't answer and just looked at her as if she had lapsed into monosyllabic gibberish, she added, "For your mother. You said you were getting a dog for your mother, remember?"

Now her question made sense. But he'd mentioned the dog over an hour ago, before they had gone in to question the bartender.

"Boy, talk about your long pauses." Josh laughed. "That almost came out of nowhere."

It was all connected in her head. She didn't see why he was having such a hard time with it. "Well, talking about the dog in your mother's future didn't exactly seem appropriate while we were questioning that bartender about a homicide right behind the club where he works," she told Josh, then got back on track. "So? Have you decided what kind you're getting?"

He hadn't gone much beyond the fact that he *was* getting his mother a canine companion sometime in the near future. If she had a pet to take care of, she wouldn't have as much time to nag him about settling down and giving her grandchildren.

"I thought maybe one of those fluffy dogs," he answered.

Off the top of her head, she could think of about twenty breeds that matched that description. "Well, that narrows it down."

She'd managed to stir his curiosity. "Why are you so interested in what kind of dog I'm going to wind up giving to my mother?"

She was just trying to be helpful. "A couple of the Cavanaughs actually *don't* strap on a gun in the morning. One of them is a vet who also works with Aurora's canine division, does their routine checkups, takes care of them if they get hurt, things like that. I think her name's Patience. Anyway, I thought you might want to talk to her, ask her some questions about the best kind of dog for your mother."

That didn't sound like a half-bad idea, he supposed since he didn't really know what he was doing. When he was a kid, he'd never owned a dog, never wanted to get attached to anything after his father's death.

"Maybe I will." He flashed Bridget a grin as he sailed through a yellow light. "When I talk to her, can I tell her that her 'Cousin Bridget' sent me?"

If he was going to use every topic to make another joke about her new family, then she shouldn't have even bothered making the suggestion.

She waved a dismissive hand at her partner. "Forget I said anything."

He was silent for a moment, as if content to let the quiet in the car prevail. But he'd been chewing on something for a while now. This last display of irritation on

Bridget's part told him that his observation over the last two months was probably right. Ever since his partner had learned about the mix-up in the hospital nearly fifty years ago, a mix-up that made her a Cavanaugh instead of a Cavelli, she'd seemed somewhat preoccupied and not quite her usual self.

"This really bothers you, doesn't it?" he asked in a voice devoid of all teasing.

"You getting a dog for your mother instead of growing up and having a meaningful relationship with a woman that lasts longer than a half-time program at the Super Bowl?" she asked glibly, deliberately avoiding his eyes. "No, not really."

She'd used a lot of words to describe a topic that she supposedly didn't care about, but that was a question to explore some other time, Josh thought. Right now, he was more concerned about Bridget's state of mind regarding the recent change in her immediate family. He might get on her case from time to time, but his three-year relationship with Bridget was the longest one he'd ever had with a woman, besides his mother. Beneath the barbs, the quips and the teasing, he really did care about Bridget. Cared about her a great deal. Sometimes more than he should, he told himself. He definitely didn't like seeing her like this.

"You know damn well I'm talking about the fact that your father found out that he'd been switched at birth with another male newborn and that he—and consequently you and those brothers and sisters of yours— are really Cavanaughs."

Bridget blew out a breath as she stared straight ahead at the road. "Yeah, I know what you're talking about, I was just hoping you'd take the hint and back off." She spared him a frown. "I should have known better."

Yeah, she should have, Josh thought. "So why does this bother you so much?" he wanted to know. "I know people in the department who'd give their right arm to wake up one morning and find out that they're related to the Cavanaughs. The very name carries a lot of weight in the department. I mean, think of it, they're an entire family of law enforcement agents and not a dirty one in the lot." He wasn't saying anything that they both didn't already know. "Hell, it's like the city's own personal branch of Camelot."

"So what's your point?" she asked, annoyed.

Driving into the parking lot of an apartment complex, Josh brought the car to a stop in the first empty space he saw.

"My point is, what's the problem you seem to be having with this?" he asked.

He was a guy. She didn't expect him to understand. Hell, she could barely understand all the tangled emotions herself. This unexpected twist made her life seem so confused, so jumbled up. There were times when she didn't know what to think, what to feel.

"The problem, oh insensitive one, is what do I do about my 'old family?' Uncle Adam, Uncle Tony, Aunt Angie, Aunt Anna." She went down the list of the people she'd believed until two months ago were her father's brothers and sisters. "Are they just strangers to me now? What *are* they to me and to the others?" she demanded with frustration. "Not to mention what are they to my dad? How am I supposed to regard them now that I know we're not blood relatives?" she asked, frustrated.

Everything had turned upside down for her. She couldn't be laid-back about the whole thing, the way her older brother Tom was. For her, all this had brought up real questions, real concerns. Moreover, it had left her with a dilemma on her hands that she had no idea how to resolve. Who *was* her family?

Josh still didn't really see what the problem was. Maybe because, in a remote way, he'd found himself in the same sort of position, except that in his case, the positions had been reversed. He'd lost his real father and found himself on the receiving end of a whole handful of generous "fathers."

"Well, speaking for myself, the word 'family' doesn't strictly refer to people with the same blood in their veins as you. After my dad was killed, a lot of his old buddies made it a point to come around to check on my mom and me to see if we were okay. The lot of them took turns looking out for us. After a while, it was like having five surrogate fathers around. They weren't my dad and they couldn't take my dad's place, but they did help to fill the void he left. They were the ones who got my mother through those dark times. I loved the lot of them and I think of all of them as family.

"The uncles and aunts you started out with before all this came to light are still your uncles and aunts in spirit if not in the strict definition of that according to the law. And let's face it, the way you feel about a person is all that counts."

Bridget looked at her partner for a long, silent moment, more impressed than she wanted to let on. "That's pretty profound coming from you. I guess even a stopped clock has to be right twice a day."

He grinned. Now *that* was the Bridget he knew and loved. "I have my moments," he acknowledged.

"Yeah," she agreed with a half smile. "Every twenty years or so, you do."

"Have you thought about talking to your Uncle Adam about how you feel about this? I mean, he is a priest and all and they're supposed to be able to offer guidance when one of their 'flock' has an emotional crisis to deal with." He raised his eyebrows in a unified query. "Right?"

She shook her head, vetoing the idea. "It might feel a little weird for both of us, considering that he's part of that crisis."

"He might surprise you."

"Two surprises in one day? I don't think I could handle that," she said flippantly. "Having you actually make sense is earth-shaking enough for me to try to come to terms with. Going for two might be asking for trouble. Who knows, the next thing that might happen is I'll be hearing the hoofbeats of the four horsemen."

Getting out of the car, he looked around the sprawling, newly upgraded complex. "I'd rather settle for that than what we're about to do next," he murmured under his breath.

They'd arrived at the apartment complex that was listed as Karen Anderson's last known residence. A residence the serial killer's latest victim had shared with her boyfriend.

Remaining beside the car, Josh scanned the area more intently, searching for apartment number 189. He was in no hurry to find it and in less of a hurry to do what he had to do.

His feet felt glued to the asphalt.

"Poor guy doesn't know what's about to hit him," he muttered grimly. Spotting a map of the area posted behind glass and next to the mailboxes, he made his way over to it. Bridget followed. "His girl goes out without him for a night out on the town and comes back dead."

"Ordinarily, if this didn't have the Lady Killer's MO all over it, I would have reminded you that your 'poor guy' would most likely be considered a person of interest. First rule of thumb in a homicide investigation, remember?" she said glibly.

"Thanks," Josh said with a touch of sarcasm. "I didn't know that." And then he grew a little more serious. "He still might be a person of interest, you know," Josh speculated.

That caught her by surprise. "You think this guy's our serial killer?"

"No." He doubted if they would get this lucky this early in this year's cat-and-mouse game with the Lady Killer. "But I think he might have taken advantage of the fact that there was a Valentine serial killer on the loose the last two years, done his homework and done away with his freewheeling girlfriend by copying the serial killer's MO. It's not like that hasn't been done before," he reminded her, "hiding a murder in the middle of a bunch of other murders."

Bridget nodded. The theory did make a lot of sense—as if they needed the extra confusion. "Just when I start to think of you as just another handsome face, you actually have a thought and blow everything out of the water," she pretended to lament.

"I am another handsome face," he acknowledged teasingly, "but I also like keeping you on your toes,

Cavanaugh." The moment the surname had slipped out of his mouth, he slanted a look at her face, waiting to see—or hear—her reaction.

As expected, she frowned—but not as deeply as he thought she might.

"Don't call me that yet," she requested. "Not until I get used to the sound of it. Deal?"

"Deal," he echoed. "Whatever you want." And then he pretended to be feeling her out. "Is it okay to call you Bridget?"

Bridget laughed and shook her head. Leave it to Josh to lighten the moment. It was a quality she really liked in him. "That's not about to change, so yeah, you can call me Bridget."

"The apartment's over in that direction," he announced, pointing to an area to their left. "It's just after the duck pond."

"Duck pond?" she echoed.

"That's what it says on the map. Looks more like a duck puddle if you ask me," he declared as they walked by it. "One way or another, we need to get this over with sooner than later."

She completely agreed. She never liked putting off anything just because she found it unpleasant to deal with. "Man after my own heart."

Leading the way, Josh turned and looked at her over his shoulder and winked. "You should be so lucky."

The wink sent a ripple through her that she deliberately ignored. "Ha! The luck," she fired back, happy to be bantering with him again, "would be all yours." What they did, day in, day out, was dark enough. A little lightness was more than welcome.

He probably would be the lucky one in this, he

thought. If he were in the market for something stable and permanent—

Which he wasn't, he reminded himself firmly before his mind could go wandering.

This wasn't the time.

They stopped in front of the ground-floor garden apartment door with the appropriate numbers affixed on it and rang an anemic-sounding bell.

When no one answered, they rang it again.

Bridget raised her hand to try ringing the bell for a third time when the door suddenly opened.

"Finally decide to come home?" a deep, humorless male voice asked. "What's the matter, lose your key again? Or did you throw it away?"

Both questions came from a semi-wet man wearing a bath towel precariously wrapped around his rather lean hips. He was standing in the doorway and his eyes filled with wonder as he looked at them with surprise. He stopped drying his hair.

His demeanor changed instantly and his expression darkened.

"Hey, I'm not giving to anything or converting to anything so go bother someone else," he said curtly. With that the man grabbed the doorknob and started closing the door.

Josh put his foot in the way and effectively provided an immovable object that stopped the other man from closing the door.

"We're not selling anything," he told the other man. "Are you James King?"

"Yeah," the man answered, his eyes shifting suspiciously from one to the other. "Who are you?"

Bridget took out her badge and ID at the same time that Josh did.

Josh made the introductions. "I'm Detective Young-blood. This is Detective Cavelli." He'd faltered for a second, then decided, in order to avoid any confusion, to state the name that she still had printed on her iden-tification. "We'd like a few words with you. Mind if we come in?"

The man remained standing exactly where he was. The suspicion deepened on his face. "What's this all about?" he demanded.

"Mr. King, really, this will be a lot easier on every-one if we step inside your apartment. You're not going to want to hear this standing out here like this, half naked," Bridget told him, her voice taking on a gentle note.

After a moment, the man took a step into his apart-ment, opening the door wider so that his unexpected visitors could enter.

Chapter 4

Looking somewhat perturbed and confused about this unexpected invasion, King turned around just as Josh closed the door to the apartment behind them.

"Look, I just got home from the gym and I was taking a shower when you started leaning on my bell," he told them irritably. "You mind if I get dressed first before you ask whatever it is you're here to ask?"

"No. As a matter of fact, I'd highly recommend it," Bridget replied as the man tugged his sagging bath towel back up to his waist.

King looked slightly amused at her answer. For a moment, it seemed as if he forgot he was annoyed and transformed into a player right before her eyes. "Really? Most women don't say that to me."

It was Josh's turn to be annoyed. He didn't particularly like the way the victim's so-called boyfriend was eyeing Bridget. He moved forward, placing himself between King and his partner. "What are you doing going to the gym in the middle of the day? Don't you have a job you're supposed to be at?"

King had already walked into his bedroom to get dressed. He left the door open; whether it was as an invitation or just to be able to hear better wasn't clear.

"Not anymore," the man bit off. "My company decided to relocate to Utah last month—without me." There was a bitter note in his voice. "I've got to do something to keep myself occupied during the day so I go to the gym. I've got seven months left on the membership. No sense in letting it go to waste," he retorted defensively. It was obvious that this wasn't the first time he'd been asked about his free afternoons.

King walked back into the living room where he'd left them. He wore a pair of beige slacks and a light green golf shirt. He was still barefoot and he hadn't bothered to try to towel dry his wet hair.

"Look, what's this all about, anyway?" he asked, looking from one to the other. "Is this Karen's idea of some kind of a joke?"

"Why would you think that?" Bridget asked. It seemed to her rather an odd thing for the victim's boyfriend to think, especially since they hadn't told him anything yet. Just what sort of a relationship did King and the dead woman have?

"I dunno. Maybe she thinks sending over two pretend cops might get me to find a job faster. Well, it can't. I already told her, there's nothing out there. I've been looking my butt off and I can't find anything decent to even apply for," he answered angrily.

Bridget didn't bother pointing out that they weren't

"pretend cops." He would realize they were real soon enough. "You didn't go out with her last night."

She didn't make it sound like a question, but he answered it anyway. "We had a fight."

"About what?" Josh asked.

"Aren't you paying attention?" King demanded, clearly annoyed at the interrogation. "About me not working. She hates it," he complained. "Karen earns a boatload of money at that place she works, but she wants me to be paying all the bills. She thinks that's what a 'real man' is supposed to do." He sneered at the very thought. "Well, the hell with that and the hell with her!"

Josh continued asking questions. He kept his voice mild, as if they were just having a harmless conversation instead of King just possibly painting himself into a corner. "Just how heated did the argument get between you two yesterday?"

King shrugged, as if this was nothing new. "We got a little loud, she threw a few things at me, missed, then stormed out." And then King narrowed his eyes, asking a little uneasily, "Why? Where is Karen?"

"Didn't you wonder that before now?" Bridget asked, curious.

King's temper flared. He was the kind of man who didn't like to be questioned about his behavior. "I thought she crashed at one of her girlfriends' places. Frankly, I liked the peace and quiet for a change."

What a bastard, Bridget thought. This was why she steered clear of relationships. It was all sweetness and fun in the beginning. And then the gloves came off and people started to be themselves—people she could very well live without. Or at least that's the way it had been with the few relationships she'd had. Most of the time, the guys either wanted her to stop being a cop—or they wanted to handcuff her with her own cuffs. Which was why she was currently taking a break from dating altogether.

"That's good," she told him coolly, "because that's something you're going to have to get used to." *Unless the county decides you killed her and then you'll be getting a whole bunch of new roommates.*

"What are you saying?" King demanded, letting his temper flare. "Where is she? Where's Karen? Something happen to Karen?" he asked, the tone of his voice taking on an unsteady lilt.

Bridget exchanged looks with Josh.

One of them would have to tell the annoying man the woman he'd just been ranting about was dead. She decided to spare Josh since he'd just made her realize that it brought back such harsh memories for him of the time he and his mother had been on the receiving end of those awful words.

"Mr. King, I'm sorry to have to be the one to tell you this, but your girlfriend was found dead this morning in the alley behind The Warehouse Crowd," Bridget told him. She assumed the victim's boyfriend was familiar with the club that was predominantly frequented by an under-thirty crowd.

King looked utterly stunned as he stared at her. "Dead?" He repeated the word as if he didn't quite understand what it meant. His breathing grew noticeably more shallow and faster as he asked, "You mean like in a homicide?"

"Exactly like in a homicide," Josh confirmed for King. Dark brown eyes went from one to the other like marbles pushed to and fro by the wind. King still appeared dazed, but anger began to etch its way into his features.

"Who did it?" he asked. "Do you know who did it?" This time, it was a demand.

"Not yet, but that's what we're trying to figure out by piecing things together," Bridget told him, doing her best to sound sympathetic even as she was still trying to make up her mind about King. "Do you know if Karen had any enemies, any old boyfriends who didn't take kindly to being dumped by her?"

"We've been together for three years. There *are* no boyfriends," King said vehemently. "And she didn't have any enemies. Karen could be a pain in the butt sometimes, but then she'd turn around and be this sweet, amazingly thoughtful woman who made you feel glad just to be alive and around her. Everyone liked Karen," he insisted. King suddenly looked stricken, as if what he'd been told was finally sinking in. His voice became audibly quieter as he asked, "She's not coming home?"

Bridget shook her head as sympathy flooded through her. "I'm afraid not."

His knees giving way, King sank down on the cream-colored sofa. He dragged his hands through his hair, distraught. "Last thing I said to her was I didn't want her coming back," he confessed brokenly.

"We can't ever know that the last thing we say to someone is going to be the last thing we ever say to that person," Josh told him. Maybe if people had the ability to have that sort of insight, they'd be a whole lot nicer to one another, he thought.

"Is there anyone you want us to call for you?" Bridget asked him.

King shook his head, struggling to pull himself together and save face. "No, I can call." And then his voice broke again as he asked, "Did she suffer?"

"ME said it was quick," Bridget was fast to assure him. "Can you tell us where Karen worked? We'd like to ask her coworkers some questions."

He gave them the name and address of a firm that handled event planning for the rich and famous called The Times of Your Life. Thanking him, Bridget gave him one of her business cards and asked him to call if he could think of anything else.

"The ME hasn't seen her yet, remember?" Josh said as they left the apartment and walked back to the car. "You said so yourself."

"Yeah, I know," she responded with a dismissive sigh. "But I didn't see the point in burning the image of the killer carving out her heart while she was still alive into his head. Knowing the bloodthirsty media, King'll find out about that soon enough."

Josh looked at her just before he got into the vehicle. "So you believe him?"

She hedged for a moment, wanting to get his take on it first. "Don't you?"

"Actually, yeah, I do. But you're usually the overly suspicious one," Josh reminded her. He found that unusual. In his experience, the softer sex tended to be more trusting. But then, he'd come to learn that there were a lot of amazing, unique things about his partner. She was a woman of substance. "You should have been the one named Thomas in your family, not your brother. As in Doubting Thomas."

Bridget rolled her eyes. "Yes, I'm familiar with that term, thank you," she said briskly. "King looked genuinely broken up when I told him that his girlfriend was dead," she explained as she got in on the passenger side.

Josh didn't know how King had actually felt about the victim in the long run, but he could see why the man had been initially overwhelmed. "It's always harder when the last words you've had with someone were angry or deliberately hurtful."

"You sound like you speak from experience."

"Me?" Her comment caught him off guard. "No," he said with feeling. "That's why I believe in amiable breakups." He started up the car. "Always leaving 'em smiling is my motto."

Leaving being the key word there. The man had trouble written all over him, she thought, not for the first time.

Bridget noted the wide grin on his face as he told her his "motto." Knowing Youngblood, there was only one way to read that. She tried not to dwell on the image of him that raised in her mind. "That's a little bit too much information, Youngblood."

He laughed heartily. "Why, Detective, you have a dirty mind."

"Three years partnered with you will do that to a person," she assured him.

"Can't plant a seed and have it grow where there is no dirt," Josh countered glibly.

"Dirt being the operative word here," Bridget said pointedly.

Josh glanced at the clock on the dashboard. It was getting close to noon. "You want to pass through a drive-through and grab some lunch on the way to this events-planning place?" he asked.

Looking at the dashboard clock herself, Bridget sighed. It was now or who knew when? "What I'd like is to stop someplace and eat lunch slowly at a table like a normal person, but, since that's impossible and in the interest of time, your way's probably better."

"My way's always better," Josh cracked. He gave Bridget a choice of several places that were close by and she picked one. Nodding amiably, he began to drive in that direction. "Why do you think he does it?" he asked as he merged into the left-hand lane. He needed to make a left turn at the next light.

When he plucked conversations out of the air like that, he managed to completely lose her. She could feel her temper growing short.

"Who?" she asked

"The Lady Killer," Josh elaborated. "What do you think his driving force is? Why February? Is he making some kind of a macabre statement about Valentine's Day, or does the guy just hate a really short month?" he ended wryly.

"You mean is he killing women to make some kind of a protest against commercialism?" she asked incredulously.

"I think if that were the case, he could have found a more subtle way to get his point across," she told Josh. "My guess is that someone jilted him, and I mean royally, and unlike a lot of people, he couldn't handle the embarrassment of it." Her mind raced as she fleshed out her theory, trying to find the pieces that fit. "Maybe he's this invisible guy and he got tired of no one really seeing him. This is his way of getting even with the woman."

"And every woman who reminds him of her," Josh speculated.

Bridget nodded, agreeing. But there was a slight problem with that theory. "But why just in February?" she asked Josh. "Why isn't he killing women all year round, every time he sees someone who looks like the woman who broke his heart?"

Josh laughed shortly. The caseload would be absolutely impossible if that were the case. "Whose side are you on?"

"Ours," she told him with feeling. "I'm just trying to get into the guy's head and figure out what motivates him. That way, we can finally get him." She couldn't think of anything she wanted more for Valentine's Day than to get this psycho off the streets of her city.

As he drove to their destination, Josh reviewed what she'd just said when she started using him as a sounding board. Something she'd just thrown out had stuck. "My guess would be that he's doing it in February because that was when she rejected him, during all the hype and commercialism leading up to the 'big day.' Department stores, restaurants, greeting card companies, they're making a big deal of Valentine's Day these days. Subtly or blatantly they make a person feel like there's something wrong with them if they don't have someone special by their side on that day."

He seemed to have a pretty good lock on all the hoopla surrounding the day, Bridget thought. That had her entertaining other questions about her partner. She told herself that she was only being curious about a friend, but even she knew that there was more to it than that. But exactly what she was not about to go into or explore. That would be asking for trouble.

"Speaking of which," she began on a much lighter note, "who's going to be by your side on Valentine's Day? Since your cell phone hasn't rung in, oh, the last two hours, I'm assuming that you and—Linda, was it?—are now officially history." That was the way he operated. Hot and heavy for a few days and then he'd start craving the sweet taste of freedom. She felt truly sorry for any woman who really fell in love with Josh. Luckily that wouldn't be her.

"Don't worry about who I'm going to be with," he told her, flashing his thousand watt-smile. "And you know damn well her name was Linda."

Was. I was right, Bridget thought with a quick flare of satisfaction.

"I'm not worried," she informed him, "just curious. And as for my reaching for a name to your last current squeeze, there've been so many women in and out of your life these last three years that it's hard for me to keep track of their names."

He looked at her pointedly, "No one asked you to keep track."

"You're my partner," she answered matter-of-factly. "If someone finds you strangled and naked in your bed bright and early one morning, I want to know who to go looking for."

Stopping at a light, he took the opportunity to turn toward her and study her for a moment. "You think of me that way a lot?"

"What, strangled?"

He grinned. He knew that *she* knew he wasn't referring to that. "No, naked and in bed."

"No, but I do I think of you strangled a lot." Changing the subject quickly before the color of her complexion changed and gave him something else to tease her about, Bridget nodded toward the drive-through he was approaching. Because it was still the early part of the lunch hour, there were five cars already queued up ahead of them.

"Why don't we just go in and order?" she suggested. She didn't relish the idea of being stuck in a line, idling. "It'll probably be a lot faster and it'll waste less gas."

"Sensible," he agreed. He'd never admit it to her, but it was one of the things he admired about his partner. She didn't just go with the easy answers; she liked to think things through. "How is it that no one's snapped you up yet, Bridget?" he teased.

"Just lucky I guess," she countered dryly as he pulled into an empty parking spot. He put the car into "park" and then turned off the ignition.

"No sense in the two of us going in." Josh opened the door on his side. "I'll go," he volunteered, then paused before getting out. "What do you want?"

"For the Lady Killer to come down with a quick, terminal disease and die before Valentine's Day. But I'll settle for a beef burrito and a diet cola," she concluded philosophically.

"Amen to the first part," Josh responded glibly. "I'll be right back with lunch." With that he got out and shut the door behind him.

Bridget tried to relax for a moment. She leaned the back of her head against the headrest, willing the tension out of her body.

Without realizing it, she watched her partner as he walked toward the restaurant's entrance and mused—

not for the first time—that Josh had a really cute butt for someone who could, at times, be a real pain in the exact same area.

One of life's mysteries, she supposed.

Their long afternoon, spent talking to Karen's co-workers at The Times of Your Life, turned out to be as fruitless as their morning had been before it. They returned to the squad room with nothing more to go on than they already had when they first left. The victim, everyone had sworn, was someone who no one would have wanted to hurt.

Until someone had.

Bridget sat back and stared at her handiwork. The bulletin board was filled with the photographs and names of all of the Lady Killer's previous unfortunate victims. And now Karen Anderson had unwillingly joined their ranks.

What were they missing?

Ten red-haired young women in their twenties all stared back at her, their smiles frozen in time, all silently begging to be avenged and to have their killer stopped and brought to justice.

Who the hell is he and how can he possibly sleep at night? she asked herself.

In the next breath, she silently mocked herself for even asking the question. The Lady Killer undoubtedly slept just fine because he did not operate by the same set of rules that the rest of them did.

As normal people did.

Because he wasn't normal.

That was the big thing she had to remember. The

Lady Killer thought and reacted on a far different plane from that of either she or Josh.

"He got started early this time," Bridget realized, thinking out loud. She could feel Josh watching her, so she elaborated for his benefit. "This is February second. Most likely he killed Karen last night, which was the first day of the month. Last year we didn't find a body until the eighth."

He remembered. The maimed body behind the gas station store. The girl had just turned twenty the week before.

"Didn't mean that there wasn't one," he pointed out grimly.

She didn't agree. "No, this guy likes to show off his handiwork. It's like he's bragging, telling us we can't catch him. That he's smarter than we are." She turned away from the bulletin board and looked at Josh. "Maybe it's someone who washed out from the academy?"

Josh tried to follow her line of thinking. "So he's showing us that he can get away with murder to make us pay for not hiring him?" Saying it out loud made it seem really far-fetched.

She didn't want to let go of the new angle just yet, but it belonged in a different light.

"No, he's reliving getting even with the woman who turned him down—that's his primary driving force. But every which way he turns, he gets rejected. His feelings toward the police department might be no different from what he feels for the woman who turned him down. Thumbing his nose at the efforts of the police to find him might just be a big bonus feature for him."

Josh turned it over in his head. "Worth a shot, I

guess," he agreed. "But if we're going to go through old files," which was what he assumed she was getting at, "we're going to need some extra people and the budget's tight."

He wasn't telling her anything she didn't already know. Lieutenant Howard had made a point of letting them all know that there was no more money for overtime but if extra hours needed to be put in, he expected that to be done—with no extra compensation.

"Don't worry. If Howard says no to putting at least a couple of extra people on this, I know who to ask," she promised. "Someone who can see beyond a dollar sign and fostering his own 'legend.'"

Josh grinned. He didn't have to ask what she was thinking. "That's my girl."

A quick, warm salvo shot through her in response to his words and the way he looked at her as he said it before she had a chance to shut it down.

What the hell was *that* all about? she upbraided herself impatiently.

She didn't have time for this.

Chapter 5

"You think I'm going to endanger my career by going out on a limb and authorizing overtime for you and your little playmate here just so that you can find some dirt to tarnish the police department's good name in the community?" Lieutenant Howard demanded. His voice rose in direct correlation to the pulsating blue vein that snaked its way along his forehead.

It amazed Bridget just how obstinate her new acting supervisor could be. Determined to cross her *t*'s and dot her *i*'s, she had gritted her teeth and deliberately gone through the proper channels—in this case, that would be Howard—to make her request for more manpower. They needed help to plow through the mountain of files she was anticipating—once she and Josh began going over all the academy's rejects from three to five years ago.

The request had momentarily stunned the preening lieutenant into complete silence. He'd come out of his office to ask for a status report on the investigation, apparently expecting to hear that they were closing in on a suspect. Instead, he'd been hit with a request for exactly what he'd already told his squad he had no intentions of allowing.

The vein across his forehead pulsed harder.

The second he'd opened his mouth, the very faint hope that he might actually be reasonable and consider her request went down in flames. Bridget had to admit that it wasn't exactly a surprise.

Well, at least no one could accuse her of going over the man's head without first giving him a chance to work with her.

Still, she felt she had to straighten out Howard's misconception. "No, not overtime. I'm asking for extra people. And it's not to make the department look bad, it's to find out who the department was intuitive enough not to hire in the first place."

Bridget searched the lieutenant's face for some indication that she'd gotten through. There was none. Apparently her words weren't penetrating the force field around his brain.

"The answer's no. You and Youngblood put in whatever time you have to get this guy behind bars, and you do it because you're supposedly good cops, not because you think you're going to line your pockets and your buddies' pockets with extra cash." Drawing himself up to his full five feet ten inches, Howard glared down at her. "Now, did I make myself clear?"

She met his glare without flinching or looking away.

Bridget was not easily intimidated, thanks to growing up with four brothers.

"Perfectly," she bit off.

"Good. Now get this damn case solved and off my desk, and I mean like *yesterday,* you hear me?" Howard ordered. Then, fuming, he turned to go back to his office.

Bridget squared her shoulders, hating the fact that she'd gotten a dressing-down in front of all the other detectives, as well as Josh. The latter was standing beside her and she could literally *feel* his anger. Despite his easygoing manner, she knew that Josh had even less regard for Howard than she did. And, whatever else his faults were, the man was protective of her, as she was of him. It was one of the reasons they worked so well together.

"People on the first floor can hear you," she answered under her breath, but not exactly as quietly as she could have.

Howard's back stiffened and spun around on his heel. Five strides brought him back to her.

"What was that?" he demanded angrily, glaring down at her.

"I said I hear you, Lieutenant," she replied, doing her best to sound calm as she raised her eyes to his.

He appeared to weigh his options as he slanted a glance around the immediate area. She could almost hear what he was thinking. That the squad room was too full for him to say what he wanted to say to her. She had a feeling that he'd save it for another time when he had her alone in his office.

"Damn straight you hear me," he finally bit off curtly. "Just because you found out you have some kind of made-up connection to the chief of detectives, don't think that makes you entitled to any special treatment. It doesn't mean a damn *thing* in my book."

As the lieutenant ranted, she realized that Josh had risen to his feet behind the man and was about to confront him. Bridget got up, moving so that she managed to block her partner with her back, preventing him from easily reaching Howard.

"Now, if you know what's good for you, you'll both get to work!" Howard shouted at her, glared at Josh and then stormed away.

"He shouldn't talk to you like that," Josh growled, frustrated. "Why'd you stop me?" he asked. "That S.O.B. needs to have some sense, not to mention manners, shaken into his head."

"You won't get an argument out of me," she agreed. "But having you put on suspension or brought up on charges of insubordination isn't going to help me or teach that pompous ass anything," she pointed out. The lieutenant's ego made it impossible for him to absorb anything.

Josh shoved his hands into his pockets, fisting them as exasperation rippled through him. "Maybe not, but it sure would have felt good getting things off my chest." Fuming, Josh looked over her head toward Howard's office. The latter had closed the door behind him and now appeared to be staring at his computer.

Or, more likely, he was trying to observe them by pretending to be occupied.

Furious, Josh looked back at Bridget. "How can you be so calm?"

She wasn't calm, not by a long shot. But letting her anger show through wouldn't get her anywhere at this point, so she internalized it. Externally she was the picture of serenity.

"You know that old saying?" she asked innocently. "The one that goes, 'Don't get angry, get even'?" It was obvious that was what she had in mind.

A smile spread across Josh's lips. Just for the briefest of moments, Bridget paused, allowing herself to take in the feeling that his smile generated inside of her.

The next moment, she was aware of what she was doing and quickly tamped everything down.

Everything but her next move.

"What do you have in mind?" Josh prodded. He couldn't think of anything he would have liked better than to take Howard down a few pegs. Well, maybe a few things, but none that he could do here.

Bridget was trying very hard to move past the putdown she'd just received from the acting lieutenant. With any luck, *he* would be a thing of the past soon.

"What I should have done instead of wasting my time talking to Howard and his oversize ego."

Yes! She was finally going to see the chief of detectives, Josh thought. Given the way he knew she felt about getting things done on her own, this was tantamount to a last resort for her. His partner didn't like asking for favors or help. But this wasn't just a minor dustup; this was important. A lot was at stake here and it couldn't be placed in jeopardy just because the acting lieutenant had turned out to be a taller version of Napoleon.

"Want some backup?" he asked her.

Bridget shook her head. She didn't want him being collateral damage. "Thanks for the offer, but if this thing blows up on me, one of us needs to stay with the case to be able to get whoever gets put in my place up to speed."

"Nobody could take your place," Josh told her and although there was a smile on his lips as he said it, his voice was dead serious. She looked at him, somewhat surprised, not quite sure what to make of his tone. Or the corresponding warm feeling his words had created within her.

"Someone might have to. Howard wants my head on a pike," she pointed out.

"Doesn't matter what *he* wants," Josh assured her with conviction. He fell into place beside her as she walked out of the squad room. "I've got your back, just like always."

It wasn't a statement, it was a promise.

She didn't bother trying to talk Josh out of coming with her. Or to point out that he was putting himself out on the same limb. There were things Josh could be kidded out of and things that he couldn't. This was one of those things that fell under the latter heading.

So all she could do was say "Thanks," which she did, and pray that everything would turn out.

She prayed hard.

Chief of Detectives Brian Cavanaugh prided himself on knowing everyone who worked for him not only by sight, but by name as well. He also made it a point to be aware of their records and achievements, both good and bad. He considered them all members of his team. To Brian, they were more than just badge numbers, they were people. *His* people.

It was no small source of pride that his three sons had worked their way high up through the ranks because of their own efforts, not because of anything that he had done for them. They would have never asked him to intervene on their behalf and he would have never interfered in any matter between a detective and his or her superior—unless there was some sort of injustice.

In like manner, Brian was acutely aware of walking a very thin, narrow line every day that he picked up his shield and tucked it into his pocket. And he had sworn to himself that should the day someday come when he, knowingly or unknowingly, stepped off that narrow path, he would turn in that shield and walk away.

He was proud of the fact that, as of yet, that day had not arrived. He was determined that it never would.

Lost now in thought, searching for a word that persisted in eluding him, a noise penetrated through the fog around him. Brian glanced up from his report. The knock on the door seemed designed to give him a reprieve, however minor. He took it gladly.

Rotating his shoulders to alleviate some stiffness, he called out, "Come in."

The next moment, he saw Bridget sticking her head in. She looked at him a little hesitantly.

Brian smiled warmly. He'd taken an interest in her, the way he had in a good many other detectives, when she had first gotten her shield. He'd known her to be a hard worker even before her true identity—like the identities of her siblings—had come to light for all of them. He and Bridget had exchanged a few words since her father's connection to the rest of them had become apparent, but he sensed that she wasn't comfortable in this new role fate had given her.

And now she'd come to him with something that

was obviously bothering her. He found himself growing very curious. He rose to his feet, a habit instilled in him by his mother.

"Bridget," he said warmly, her very name serving as a greeting. "Come in."

She remained in the doorway, still uncertain. "Are you busy?"

"Not for you," he assured her. And then he saw that she'd brought her partner with her. For backup? he wondered. Or was there another reason they had both come to him together? He searched his memory quickly, then remembered that while he was more than satisfied with the performance of Bridget and Josh's division, the man who had been placed temporarily in charge left a few things to be desired—such as actual leadership qualities. He believed in giving people a chance to prove themselves in new situations, but he had been far too laid-back when it came to Jack Howard. He suspected that the man really didn't belong in charge of other people. For one thing, the lieutenant lacked a very important leadership quality: empathy.

"To what do I owe this unexpected visit?" Brian asked, sitting down again behind his desk. He gestured toward the two chairs that faced his desk. "Take a seat, please."

Both she and Josh immediately did as the chief requested. Bridget placed her hands on the armrests, giving the impression that she was ready to spring up to her feet at the slightest provocation. Tension fairly radiated from her.

"It's not going as fast as we'd like," Bridget said, responding to the chief's question, measuring her words out slowly in an attempt to make sure that she wouldn't say the wrong thing. She didn't want the chief of detectives to think that she was some flighty person running to him with a complaint rather than going through proper channels.

Yet here she was, presenting her case. Proper channels were all well and good when there was a great deal of time to spare. But there wasn't. She just couldn't get away from the feeling that they—and the next victim—didn't have a great deal of time left. That their time—like the days in the month of February—was exceedingly limited.

The Lady Killer was out there somewhere, getting ready to strike again. Soon. They needed to find him before he could, they just *had* to. And if that meant ticking off the lieutenant by going over his head after he turned her down, then that was what she had to do if she was ever going to live with her conscience.

Brian leaned forward and folded his hands before him on his desk. "All right, I'm listening," he encouraged patiently.

"The fact is, Chief, we need more bodies. Live ones," she clarified when the grizzly scenario her words suggested echoed back in her head. "This particular serial killer only strikes in the month of February," she pointed out, although she had a feeling that the chief was already quite aware of that. The man was aware of *everything,* to the point that it was almost eerie.

"And if the past is any example," Josh said, picking up the thread from his partner, "with each year, he tries to increase his number of victims. The first year he killed three women, last year he killed five. This year he already killed one woman and there are twenty-seven days left to go."

There was no need to have the dots connected for him. Brian had already had his aide bring him a copy of the file on the Lady Killer. He'd gone over it first thing this morning. His breakfast had weighed heavily on his stomach by the time he'd finished reading.

"Go on," he told the two people sitting before him.

Bridget spoke up first, not because she wanted the attention, but because, if this backfired, she was ready to take the blame. And if word got back to Howard that the request had been made over his head, she didn't want Josh to be the one to take the flak. She was the lead detective on this case. Besides, Josh just might get it into his head to turn in his badge if Howard hassled him, while she would dig her heels in even further.

"We need more people working this case, sir," she stated emphatically.

"I'm in complete agreement," Brian assured her. Something like this, that had gone on for more than a year even if it was only during the length of one month each time, deserved to have the attention of more than just two detectives. The fact that it didn't raised questions. "Why *aren't* there more of you on it?" he asked.

She would have loved to bring a great many issues to his attention. There was the fact that Howard wanted to keep his budget figures reined in while demanding that all his detectives put in extra hours. That would make it appear as if cases were being solved by his division in a minimum of time since only the core hours were logged in.

There was also the fact that since Howard had come in morale had dropped to a dangerously low point. But too many complaints might come across to the chief as her being petulant. The case was too important for her to risk possibly losing the chief's goodwill.

She worded her answer as diplomatically as she could. "I don't think that the lieutenant wants it to appear as if he's exceeding his budget on some momentary whim."

Brian's eyes narrowed at the description. "Taking down a serial killer is hardly a whim in my book," he responded. "It's being a good cop." He looked from his niece to her partner. "Have you found any suspects yet?"

Bridget ran her tongue along her lips that had grown very dry in the last few minutes. "Well, in theory," she began.

"And this theory is?" Brian prodded.

Bridget blew out a breath. *Here goes nothing.* "That whoever the killer is, he might also be trying to get even with the police department, making them regret that they didn't hire him."

That was a new angle. But Brian had learned long ago not to appear surprised by anything while on the job, so, to the two people in his office, he looked as if he took this new information in stride.

His expression gave nothing away as he asked, "You think that the killer is someone who tried to get into the academy?"

"It does seem likely," Josh told him. "The killer never tried to hide any of the bodies of his victims. Instead, he always made sure to leave them out in plain sight, as if he was taunting the police with his kills."

"According to the ME's report," Bridget added, "these women were all killed late at night. Depending on where, that gave the killer plenty of time to either move the bodies where they couldn't be found or get rid of them altogether. But he didn't. It's like he *wants* the police department to see his work."

"He's rubbing our noses in it," Brian summarized.

Enthused because the chief wasn't dismissing their theory out of hand, Bridget laid out her plan. "Exactly. I'd like to go through all the old academy applications from about three, four years ago, limiting the search to strictly the ones who didn't wind up graduating for one reason or another."

Brian nodded, seeing no reason to deny her request. "Do it." He noticed the way Bridget suddenly caught her lower lip between her teeth. The unconscious action reminded him of Janelle. His daughter had the same habit when she debated whether or not to bring something to light. "What?" he asked encouragingly.

"We could certainly use some extra people to make this go faster."

Brian didn't see what the problem was. "Get them," he instructed. "Borrow them from other departments if you have to."

She searched for a way to delicately approach what she was about to say next without making it sound as if she was being disloyal to her department—or the man in charge of it. This being diplomatic was *hard*. As a rule, she liked speaking her mind, not tiptoeing through invisible minefields.

When she paused, Brian read between the lines. His days as a detective were not so far in the past that he couldn't remember what it was like to have to rein himself in and make sure he didn't get ahead of himself and step on toes that were very capable of kicking back.

"I'll inform Lieutenant Howard of my decision to

allot extra manpower for a task force. This case is long overdue for a task force," he added.

Since the unofficial "meeting" appeared to have come to an end, Brian rose to his feet. Bridget and Josh quickly followed suit.

"Thank you for filling me in on the case," Brian said amiably, walking them to the door. "And don't worry," he added conspiratorially, "your names won't come up."

Bridget paused half a second to look at him. For that split second, he wasn't the chief. Instead, for the first time since she'd learned the startling news about her father and who they all actually were, Brian Cavanaugh was her uncle. He was family, family beyond the blue uniform that made them so.

She nodded at his words. "I wasn't worried," Bridget told him.

Brian smiled. There was a great deal about this one that reminded him of the way his daughter, Janelle, had been just a few short years ago. Dedicated and so very intent on hiding any uncertainties and insecurities that she might have. Bridget, apparently, had yet to learn that those insecurities didn't diminish her and surmounting them was what made her the person she was.

"I know," he replied. And then he winked at Josh, as if taking him into his confidence, and told Bridget, "I was talking to your partner."

With that, he closed his door and returned to his desk. Before reaching for the phone to call Howard and inform the man that he wanted a task force set up and was making an allotment in the budget for it, he thought back to the partner he'd had even before he'd gone on to earn his shield.

Best damn partner anyone could ask for, he thought, the corners of his mouth curving fondly. At the time, he couldn't do anything about the way he felt. Both he and his partner, Lila, were married at the time. To other people.

But if something is meant to be, it happens, and every day he thanked God that it had happened to him.

Wouldn't surprise him if Bridget and her partner wound up the same way. They had that look about them, even if they didn't realize it yet.

Brian dialed Howard's extension and sat back in his chair.

Chapter 6

"I'd really watch my step if I were you, Bridget."

The word of warning, uttered in a raspy low voice by Gary Cox, one of three detectives who had been loaned out to her division for the duration of the Lady Killer investigation, had Bridget looking up from her computer uncertainly. Cox had paused by her desk on the pretext of searching for something in the file he was holding.

"What do you mean?" she asked quietly.

His eyes still down, Cox pushed his rimless reading glasses up on the bridge of his nose. It was a losing battle. "I've worked with Jack Howard before the guy was kicked upstairs and made lieutenant. Thinks nothing of throwing people under the bus if that somehow helps elevate him or gets him seen in a better light. I hear you're the reason this task force exists. That can't sit well with him."

"You know better than that, Cox," Josh said mildly, coming up behind his partner and facing the other detective. "Cavelli is a detective, same as you and me. A lowly detective doesn't have the clout to get a task force put together. That kind of authority has to come from on high."

Cox looked at them knowingly. "My point exactly. You went over Jack Howard's head—not that anyone could blame you," he added quickly. "Man's a show-boating jackass. But that doesn't change the fact that he's gonna be watching every move you make."

Bridget nodded, accepting Cox's words for what they were: a friendly warning. "Then I'd better make sure that all my moves are entertaining," she told him with a bright smile.

Cox pushed his glasses up his long, thin nose again. "Yeah," he agreed, an appreciative note in his voice as his eyes quickly gave her frame a once-over. "I don't think that'll be much of a problem for you. Right, Youngblood?" he asked, glancing over to her partner.

Josh wasn't smiling. "Don't you have files to go through?" he asked the older man. "Because if you're done with your share, I've got a ton more for you to review, seeing as how you're so quick and all."

Cox held his hands up in blatant surrender. "I'm going, I'm going," he protested cheerfully. "I meant no offense," were his parting words.

Bridget turned her chair halfway around so that she could get a better look at Josh. The irritated note in his voice was unlike him. She knew if she said that, it would only get her partner's back up, so instead she resorted to a general observation.

"You sound like someone who's in real need of a coffee break."

In response he raised the two tall, covered containers he had brought back with him from the shop across the street. She'd been so preoccupied, she hadn't even noticed he had them, Bridget realized. She needed to relax herself.

"What I need—what *we* need," Josh emphasized, "is a break in the case."

"No argument there." The man was preaching to the choir. "But with all these extra people helping out, we're bound to make headway a lot faster than just on our own."

"We'd better, or else Howard's going to want our blood," Josh said.

Placing Bridget's coffee—extra light, extra sugar; he had no idea why she bothered calling it coffee—container on her desk, he went around to his own desk and planted himself in his chair. He removed the lid and took a long sip of the midnight-black brew. He could feel his pulse speed up even as the dark, hot liquid wound its way down his throat and into his bloodstream.

"My blood," Bridget corrected her partner. "Cox is right. The lieutenant knows that I'm the one who asked the chief for help."

He looked at her over the rim of the large container, wisps of steam rising up into the air like a magical genie that had just been released.

"As I recall," he said pointedly, "there were two of us in the chief's office the other day."

She grinned. At times, the man was downright sweet, although she knew he'd really balk at that description when it was applied to his professional life. But that didn't make it any less true.

"Only because you insisted on tagging along," she reminded him. "I'm the one who made the request to the chief and I'm the one who'll take the fall." Her blue eyes seemed to crinkle as she added, "But thanks for the thought."

"Maybe if you stop grandstanding for a minute, you'll realize that as long as we stick together, Howard'll have a harder time getting back at us."

She leaned back in her chair for a moment and studied her partner. At one time, she might have resented his comment, which implied she couldn't look after herself. That wasn't the case anymore. These days she trusted her instincts—and her partner.

"You really do have a big-brother complex, you know that?"

The way he looked at her in response sent an unexpected warm shiver shimmying down her spine. "Yeah, that's what it is, a big-brother complex," Josh echoed sarcastically.

Unwilling to dissect and examine what she'd just experienced, Bridget lowered her eyes to her monitor and got back to work.

The extra detectives who had been sent over, Joel Langford, Sam Kennedy and Gary Cox, as well as she and Youngblood, had been plowing through a mountain of applications for the last three days. They pulled the ones for the applicants who had washed out or been rejected outright and subjected them to closer scrutiny. Each form dictated a follow-up.

A number of the failed applicants had moved on and had either left the area or the state entirely. They were set aside, reducing the numbers a little. But that still left a fairly large number of would-be police officers to contend with. Each one had to be interviewed, their whereabouts on the nights in question verified. Bridget came in early and stayed late, compiling the list of former academy candidates to interview. Once it was put together, the real work began.

"You get the feeling that this is getting us nowhere?" she asked Josh as the third day saw them wearily walking away from yet another one-time hopeful police academy applicant who ultimately hadn't been able to make the grade.

Finding the former applicants hadn't been easy and talking to them had gotten them nowhere. Many were still resentful at being rejected. Others were suspicious as to why they were being sought out at this date.

All in all, Bridget knew of far more pleasant ways to spend her time.

"It *was* a good idea," Josh told her, too tired to be very convincing despite the fact that he did believe what he was saying. "The odds of us finding the serial killer right off the bat are so astronomically low that I can't even come up with a qualifying number. But just because we haven't found him yet doesn't mean that you were wrong to think he'd washed out of the academy."

If this kept up, she would have to start checking Youngblood's ID periodically. "What's with you lately?" she asked as she got back into the car. "You're not usually this encouraging—not," she quickly added, "that I don't appreciate it."

Josh shrugged, securing his seat belt. "Figure you have enough to deal with right now, what with Howard breathing down your neck and…" His voice suddenly trailed off.

"And?" Bridget repeated, turning to look at him as she waited.

"And that identity crisis thing you said you were having."

Bridget knew he meant well, but she still didn't really want to have the subject brought up. "Never called it an identity crisis."

For a second, he left his key in the ignition and just talked. "Okay, whatever it is that has you wondering who you are."

She took offense at what he was saying. "I know who I am," Bridget protested. "I just don't know what last name I can use in good conscience."

He laughed to himself as a thought occurred to him. His eyes met hers. Hers contained a question. "Why not be like those rock stars who go by one name?" he teased. Then, assuming a deep voice like the one that might be heard making a TV promo, Josh said, "And now, here's *Bridget*." He accompanied the single name with a sweeping gesture of his hands.

Bridget shook her head. "Sorry, it's just not unique enough."

"Maybe not the name," Josh allowed. Then let his voice trail off.

Their eyes met for a moment. Bridget realized she was holding her breath, as if she was waiting for something. Waiting for what? For him to finish his sentence? Or for something else?

She wasn't making any sense, she thought, annoyed with herself. But she did have an excuse. The hours that she'd been putting in ever since the task force was formed had been long and grueling. She was bone weary and consequently, punchy. The mind wandered when you were punchy.

At that moment, as if to further torment her, her cell phone rang.

A half a moment later, so did his.

Josh turned off the ignition he'd just turned on and fished out his phone. "Youngblood," he declared just as Bridget was saying evasively, "This is Bridget," into hers.

As the people on the other end of their respective lines relayed their messages, Bridget raised her eyes to her partner's. The look she saw in his told her that he'd gotten the same message.

There'd been another murder by the serial killer.

She closed her phone and slipped it back into her pocket. "At least we can rule out the last two guys we just talked to," she said grimly. "Although that's not much of a consolation."

"It's a start," Josh said with a resigned sigh as he turned on the ignition again.

The woman who had stumbled across the body lying in an alley behind a strip mall and had subsequently called 911 was still there when they arrived on the scene some fifteen minutes later. Sitting before the open rear doors of an ambulance, it was obvious that the young woman was very much in shock and fighting the strong desire to scream.

As they approached, the woman kept running her hands up and down her arms. Moreover, she was sitting on the floor of the ambulance, precariously perched and rocking to and fro in a vain attempt to comfort herself.

The first officer to respond to the call, treading lightly around the witness, told them that the woman's name was Alyce Jackson and that by some strange stroke of fate, she and the latest victim, Diana Kellogg, worked together.

"Diana didn't come in today," Alyce said, plucking her words out of the middle of her thoughts when Bridget and Josh asked her to tell them what happened. She pressed her lips together to keep them from trembling. It wasn't working. The woman was a bundle of nerves. "Wasn't like her to miss work and not call. She's usually so good about things like that." She looked from Bridget to Josh. "She was responsible, you know?"

Josh glanced at Bridget before saying to the distraught woman in a comforting voice, "Yes, I know the type."

"But I thought, she's young, maybe she met someone and had such a good time, she just lost track. That happens you know." There was a desperate note in her voice, as if trying to convince herself, not them.

"Was she meeting someone last night?" Bridget asked her gently.

Alyce took a deep breath before responding. "Yeah," she answered, nodding her head.

They were going to have to be careful, Bridget thought. The woman was fragile. "You know who?"

The brunette shook her head, tears shining in her

eyes. "I don't think Diana knew who, either. It was one of those dates you get set up for you online. The group was called Romantics-dot-net or dot-com or something," she said, frustrated that the exact name escaped her. "He gave her a description of himself, but said he didn't want to send her a picture. He told her that he wanted to see if she could pick him out since their souls had touched."

"How's that again?" Josh pressed, glancing at his partner uncertainly.

"Those were the words he used," Alyce insisted. "Diana repeated them to me. She thought they were so romantic." Alyce pressed her lips together again, struggling to hold herself together. "The whole thing made me a little uneasy and I offered to go with her, but she said that would really look awkward. She told me she was meeting him at a very crowded place so I shouldn't worry. But I had a feeling, I did," the woman cried, grasping Josh's hand hard with both of hers.

Struggling not to cry, Alyce paused a moment before going on. "Diana just got tired of not having someone in her life, you know?" She looked from one to the other for a sign of understanding. "And what with Valentine's Day coming, she said she was determined not to spend that day alone."

"I take it she didn't have a boyfriend?" Bridget asked the woman.

Alyce shook her head. "Not since she broke up with Alex."

Josh raised an eyebrow. Were they finally catching a break? "Alex? Who's Alex?" Maybe that was an angry ex-lover who didn't like being dumped.

"He was her fiancé." Alyce said, struggling to keep her voice from breaking.

Bridget had her notebook out. "This Alex have a last name?"

A hopeless look came over their witness's face. "Yeah, but I don't know what it is."

Josh mentally crossed his fingers. "Do you know where we can find him?"

"Texas. Dallas. That was what the breakup was all about. He wanted her to come to Dallas with him. She didn't want to leave." Alyce was crying now and didn't seem to realize it yet. "God, but I wish she'd gone with him. She'd still be alive now if she had."

Alyce raised her troubled eyes. "Do I have to look at her again?" she asked, her voice cracking and trembling. "To make an official ID, I mean. I watch procedurals on TV," she explained haltingly. "I really don't think I can handle seeing her again like that."

"No, not right now," Bridget promised, her voice calm, soothing. "Tell me, does Diana have any family or next of kin we need to notify?"

"She's got an older brother somewhere on the East Coast, I think. She never mentioned anyone local." Alyce stopped as her voice hitched. Clearing it, she tried to talk again. "How can anyone do something like that to another human being?" she asked.

"That's what we're trying to figure out," Bridget told her. Looking around, she spotted a female officer working alongside another officer as they both tried to keep the growing crowd from pushing forward and contaminating the crime scene. "Be right back," she told Josh. Hurrying over to the officer, she tapped the other woman on the shoulder. When the latter turned around, Bridget indicated Alyce. "Officer, could you go with Miss Jackson to the hospital and then once she's checked out, see she gets home all right, please?"

"Sure thing." The policewoman, Officer Mahon, seemed happy to be relieved of what she was doing. "Anything to get away from this crime scene. I'm having trouble keeping my lunch down," she confided in a lowered voice.

"We've all been there," Bridget assured the young woman.

The officer followed Bridget back to the waiting ambulance. Bridget made the introduction. "Officer Mahon is going to see to it that you get home all right after they check you out at the hospital, Alyce."

"I didn't get hurt," the woman protested. Her eyes welled up again. "Diana's the one who got hurt. Who got killed," she sobbed.

"You're in shock," Bridget told the woman softly. "We just want to make sure that you're all right," she added. "Here. If you can think of anything else, give me a call. *Anytime,*" Bridget emphasized, handing Alyce one of her cards.

"How come that argument never works with you?" Josh asked as they walked away from the ambulance and the distraught witness.

The paramedic was just getting Alyce to move onto a gurney and preparing to shut the doors so that his partner could drive to the hospital. Officer Mahon would follow them in her squad car.

Bridget looked at her own partner innocently. "What do you mean?"

"That time you were smacked in the head by that idiot who decided he was going to go into training for the L.A. Marathon right then and there, stashes of pot still hanging out of his pockets." He saw that Bridget was deliberately acting as if she didn't remember the incident. The hell she didn't, he thought. "I nearly busted a gut chasing him down. When I cuffed him and dragged him back, you looked like you had all the makings of a nasty concussion, but you utterly refused to go to the local E.R. to get yourself checked out like I kept insisting."

"There was a reason for that," Bridget replied coolly.

"And that is?" he asked, waiting for her to elaborate.

"Because I'm invulnerable," Bridget told him matter-of-factly, ending her statement with a wide, cheerful grin.

Josh sighed and rolled his eyes, then said sarcastically, "Oh yeah, I keep forgetting all about your super-powers."

She merely smiled at him as if they were having a normal, perfectly plausible conversation. "They do make a difference."

"Yeah, especially during a psych exam," Josh muttered.

The lightened mood disappeared as they went back to where the ME was just finishing up her preliminary notes. Directly next to her one of the crime scene investigators was snapping the last of his photographs.

As Bridget drew closer, both the ME and the CSI unit member became only peripheral noise to her. All she could really see or focus on was the woman lying on the ground in the alley. Like the others, her hands were folded below her carved-out chest cavity, as if she were praying.

Maybe she had been, Bridget thought grimly. For

a moment, she said nothing, merely looked. But the longer she looked, the angrier she became.

"I want this guy, Josh," she told her partner, her teeth gritted together.

"You'll have to get in line, Bridget," Josh told her. "There are a lot of relatives who feel the same way you do."

With effort, she tore her eyes away from the young woman who appeared as if she'd had everything to live for—until life was so painfully torn away from her. Bridget raised her eyes to his. "On a slab," she emphasized. "I want this guy on a slab. I want to put him there myself."

"Don't let Howard overhear you say that," Josh warned seriously. "He does, he'll accuse you of carrying on a vendetta."

"Right now," she murmured, more to herself than to her partner, "Howard is the last thing I'm worried about." She struggled not to let her emotions get the better of her. Filled with high hopes, Diana Kellogg had been slaughtered before she'd had a chance to really live.

Just like the ten victims before her.

The bastard who had done that would be made to pay for it.

She silently swore it on her mother's grave.

Chapter 7

Diana Kellogg had lived on the fourth floor of a six-story, thirty-year-old apartment building that had seen better times, not to mention a better neighborhood. While the exterior was fairly well kept up, right down to the recently trimmed juniper bushes that were vigorously growing on either side of the entrance, interior renovations did not seem have interested the landlord.

The moment Bridget and Josh walked inside, they were struck by the amount of fingerprints and smudges of dirt that seemed to litter the hallway walls. In addition, here and there, the paint had begun to peel. The smell of ammonia and disinfectant testified that the ground floor had been recently washed.

What it could really stand, though, in Bridget's opinion, was a complete replacement. Chips, holes and pockmarks seemed to be everywhere on the uninspired, jumbo black-and-white tiles.

"I'd be depressed just coming home every night," Josh commented as they made their way over to the elevator.

Since the elevator appeared to be in use, he pressed the up button and waited. A disgruntled-looking heavyset woman in her late forties came down the staircase to the left of the elevator door.

"It's broken," she told them, visibly disgusted. "Again."

Since the woman was apparently a tenant, Bridget took the opportunity to ask her, "Would you happen to know where the superintendent is?"

A contemptuous expression came over the round face. "Out back, drinking most likely."

"I'd definitely be depressed," Josh affirmed as he led the way out again. Once outside, they circled the perimeter of the building to look for the man who could let them into Diana Kellogg's apartment.

Fifteen minutes later found them inside the tiny one-bedroom apartment where Diana Kellogg had lived until last night. After getting the exceedingly curious superintendent to back out of the apartment and closing the door on him, Josh slowly looked around the living quarters.

Kellogg had done her best to make the three rooms into a home, decorating with bright, cheerful colors and inviting, comfortable furnishings, all of which acted to create a tiny haven for the young woman amid the coldness that existed just outside.

As he took in the apartment, Josh noticed that Bridget was still in the living room. He had expected her to go into the bedroom and begin rummaging through the closet the way she normally did. It was her way of getting more of a feel for the victim, her tastes, lifestyle, and so on.

But this time, she had gone directly to the laptop that had been set up on what was, beneath the pretty light blue tablecloth, a rickety card table. Turning the laptop on, Bridget waited for the computer to go through its various warming up stages until it was finally up and running. The laptop didn't appear to be a new model and the process took longer than she would have liked. The operating system was two upgrades behind the current one on the market, which contributed to the machine's less than lightning speed.

"Find anything?" Josh asked after giving the rooms a quick once-over and finding nothing noteworthy to catch his attention.

"Yeah," Bridget answered with a sigh. "That Diana Kellogg must have been an incredibly patient person. This thing is taking forever to come around," she complained, waving her hand at the laptop. "It's an old operating system."

Josh came up behind her, as if two sets of eyes watching the screen could somehow make it move more quickly.

"That's the problem," he told Bridget. "I never keep mine around for them to get that way. As soon as something new comes along, I always replace the one I have for whatever's new and faster."

"Are you talking about your computer or your love life?" Bridget deadpanned, never taking her eyes off the painfully slow-moving screen.

"Very funny," he responded. Looking closer, he saw that the laptop had finally finished loading and there was now an idyllic rainforest scene on the screen. "Hey, look, you've got a desktop," he congratulated her.

Victory went down in flames. "Yeah, but it's password protected," she observed wearily. The woman lived alone. Who was she protecting her computer from? In all likelihood, it probably only contained recipes and family photos. "We need to have one of the techs take a crack at it." About to shut the laptop down again, Bridget was surprised when her partner elbowed her out of the way. She moved, but never took her eyes off him. It wasn't exactly a hardship from her standpoint. "What are you doing?"

"Giving getting in a shot," he told her, his fingers flying across the keyboard.

"Since when did you become a hacker?"

"I'm not." The way he saw it, that was a title reserved for people who could pull virtual rabbits out of invisible hats and fish out encrypted messages with the ease that a normal person sent out email. "But this girl I dated once could crack passwords like they were so many tiny walnuts."

"Nice to know you're not wasting time just going out with pretty faces," Bridget cracked, moving back to allow him better access.

He gave her a quick, sensual look that would have melted her inner core if she'd bought into it. But she knew that Josh was just practicing his seduction skills on her, skills that he would eventually use on some other lucky young woman.

"They've got more than just pretty faces," he assured her.

"Please, spare me the details," Bridget entreated, rolling her eyes and pretending to be afraid that he was about to begin describing what each of his former girlfriends had going for them.

Focused on the laptop, Josh hit another combination of keys, then suddenly brightened. "She used the numbers of her street address. I'm in," he declared, lifting his arms in the air like a triumphant boxing champion who'd just won the world title.

"I'm sure you say that to all the girls," Bridget muttered under her breath. "Okay," she said in a louder voice, "let me take a look at her messages. Maybe we can find out what this guy's name was."

And then she saw it, the last email that the victim had opened and read before apparently leaving her apartment on her ill-fated date.

"SexyDude," Bridget read out loud. "Sounds like a bad joke."

"Or a disappointment waiting to happen," Josh commented.

"Who knows, maybe he wasn't a disappointment. Maybe he really was a 'sexy dude,'" she theorized, to which her partner simply shook his head. "Okay, why not?" she asked.

"If he actually was sexy, he wouldn't have had to advertise it," Josh said. "It would just be evident the second she met him."

And Josh would be the one to know about that, Bridget caught herself thinking. Annoyed that her thoughts had strayed so far off course, she returned her gaze to the emails that had gone back and forth between the two the last day of Kellogg's life.

"They made plans to meet at The Hideaway." She looked at Josh. "Okay, what is that?"

He laughed. "Oh, Bridget, you *are* really sheltered, aren't you? You need to get out more."

"I get out," she protested heatedly. "Just not to sleazy places."

The lopsided smile on her partner's lips told her that he didn't buy in to her protest. "The Hideaway's a club that caters to the young, single and carefree crowd."

"Maybe that should be young, single and careless crowd instead," she commented.

"Whatever," he countered with a shrug. And then he suddenly realized… "It's not too far away from the place where her body was discovered. Question is, how did SexyDude get from point A to point B without anyone noticing him and his 'extra baggage'?"

"Maybe someone did," Bridget said hopefully. She scrolled quickly through the emails that were either sent to or received from "SexyDude," looking for an attachment. There wasn't any. "Her friend was right, SexyDude didn't send her a picture." She looked up at Josh. "Ten to one SexyDude looks like a troll."

"Not taking that bet," he answered.

She'd gotten as much as she could from the laptop without some serious advanced technical help. "Okay, let's drop this laptop off with the tech department and then talk to the bartender at The Hideaway. Maybe someone remembers seeing Diana with her 'date.'"

"You really are an optimist, aren't you?" Josh commented, leading the way out.

"It's what keeps me going," she answered, shutting the door behind her.

Not only didn't the bartender remember seeing

anyone with the victim, he hadn't seen the victim, either.

The bartender, Raul Lopez, shook his head. "I've got a great eye for faces and hers wasn't here last night," he told them, tapping the photograph that Bridget had placed on the bar.

"Are you sure?" she pressed.

Raul looked as if he thought his integrity was being questioned. "I already told you, I've got an eye for faces. I don't forget them."

"All right," Josh said, placing himself so that the bartender was forced to look at him instead of at Bridget. "Let's run a little test," he proposed. "Describe my partner."

Raul didn't even hesitate. "Five-foot-seven—probably wearing three-inch heels," he guessed. "Straight, golden-blond hair, blue eyes, good skin, great smile. Late twenties. I'd put her at a hundred and ten, hundred fifteen pounds, although that bulky gray jacket she's wearing makes it hard to tell. One thing's for sure," he added, his mouth curving in a seductive grin, "she doesn't look like any police detective I ever knew. You want me to go on?" he asked Josh.

Josh was tempted to ask what else the man thought he could describe but had a feeling that it was prudent to stop here—for Bridget's sake.

"No," Josh said curtly. "You made your point. You're good with descriptions. Thanks for your time."

"Pleasure's all mine." Raul was looking at Bridget as he said it. "Come back anytime," he told her. "First drink's on me."

"Wonder what else he expects to be on him," Josh bit off as they walked out.

Bridget suppressed a grin. If she hadn't known better, she would have said her partner was being jealous. Most likely, he was just being protective. Like one of her brothers.

"So," Bridget concluded, "Kellogg never made it here." She paused as she looked over her shoulder at the club. "I wonder why."

"Maybe 'SexyDude' was waiting outside the club and waylaid her," Josh guessed. Seeing that he had his partner's attention, he continued. "Don't forget, he probably knew what she looked like. She used her real name and she had that social networking page with her photograph on it. It wouldn't have been hard to find it to see what she looked like," he added. "All the guy had to do was look her up on Google."

She kept forgetting it could be that easy. Bridget shook her head as they walked back to the car. "Such a great invention and these jerks have to ruin it by using it to 'virtually' stalk people and kill them."

There was the optimist again, he couldn't help thinking. Bridget was always trying to see the good rather than the bad. It was one of the things he liked about her. That and her mind. It also didn't hurt that she had killer legs.

Josh tamped down the grin that threatened to rise to his lips.

"Happens with everything," he said philosophically. "One of the first uses for the camera was to take what were considered to be pornographic pictures back in Edwardian times." About to get into the car, Bridget gave him a questioning look. "I read a lot," he told her. Getting in on the driver's side, he started to buckle up when he saw her taking out her cell phone. "Who are you calling?"

"Brenda," she answered. "I want to see if she managed to trace back the IP address to SexyDude's home so we can go talk to the creep."

Brenda was Brenda Cavanaugh, the wife of one of the chief of detectives' sons. He'd heard that she was an absolute wizard at what she did, but, as he glanced at his watch, this was pushing it. It had been less than an hour since they'd handed over the laptop.

"Aren't you crowding her a little? I mean, she is still human."

"Only in a very broad, general sense," Bridget deadpanned. "I've been told she's very good at her job." Because the line on the other end was being picked up, Bridget held up her hand, curtailing any further conversation with Josh for the moment.

"Brenda? Hi, this is Bridget—right, Bridget Cavanaugh." She deliberately avoided looking at Josh as she confirmed the other woman's inquiry. "Did you happen to figure out that creep's name and address yet?" The next moment, a huge smile bloomed on her face. "Terrific. I said you were the best. What is it?"

This time Bridget did raise her eyes to Josh, silently indicating that she needed something to write with and a surface to do it on. Turning his body, Josh pulled out a pen, then, because he had nothing to give her to write on, he held up his palm for her. Bridget didn't have the luxury of being choosy, so, bracing his hand with hers, she turned his palm up toward her.

The next moment, she was writing across it with his pen. "Thanks, I owe you one— What? *This* Saturday?" She let go of Josh's hand. "No, I'm not. I'm not busy. I can make it, yes. You're sure? Really? I didn't think I had one of those. Should be interesting. Okay, Josh and I will come by the lab later for anything else you can find. Bye."

Questions crowded his head by the time she got off the phone. "Didn't think you had one of what?" Josh wanted to know.

It took Bridget a second to match his question with something that she'd said previously. "Oh. That. A grandfather," she explained. Why was he asking her that? "Aren't you more interested in this creep's name?"

"Sure, but that doesn't mean I can't ask about this. You looked really surprised—and then kind of pleased—when you were talking to her and it wasn't about the case. Made me curious what could make you look like that."

"Oh, I don't know. Maybe a partner who keeps his mind on his work and hell-bent on catching the bad guy," she retorted.

And then Bridget sighed as she leaned back in the seat. Josh would find a way to wheedle this out of her one way or another and if she got it over quickly, then they could focus on what was important. Bringing that bastard to justice.

"Brenda said that Andrew—*Uncle* Andrew," Bridget amended since the man *was* family, "got a call from his father in Florida. Seems that the patriarch of the family is flying home for the express purpose of meeting this lost branch of the family that has suddenly surfaced and Andrew is spreading the word that he wants everyone to gather together for the old man."

"And the lost branch of the family, that would be you?" Josh guessed.

"Not me specifically," she protested. "It means my whole family."

"Of which you're a part." He was stating the obvious and he knew it, Bridget thought. She'd forgotten how irritating he could be at times. "By the way," Josh continued and she braced herself, "I heard you identify yourself as Bridget Cavanaugh. Does that mean you've made your decision about which last name you want to use?"

It hadn't really been her decision to make, she thought. It had actually been a foregone conclusion from the get-go.

"That means," she told him, "I can't fight City Hall, and if my father was born a Cavanaugh, I guess that makes me one, too."

He found her resigned tone amusing. "It's not exactly a death sentence. you know."

"I know. It just feels weird, that's all." She searched for a way to make him see her point. "It's like all your life, you think of yourself as a duck and suddenly, you find out that you're actually a goose. It takes some getting used to."

He laughed quietly to himself and then told her, "Swan."

She didn't understand. "What?"

"Don't think of yourself as a goose," he told her. "Think of yourself as a swan. It might make the transition easier for you."

Just what was he reading into her words? "I'm not vain—" she protested.

He cut her off before she could get going. "Never said that."

"Besides, swans have bad dispositions." She looked at him pointedly.

Josh shrugged innocently. "Just trying to help," he told her.

"You want to help?" She turned his hand so that he could see his palm with the writing on it. "Drive here," she instructed and then, belatedly, let go of his hand so that he could use it to drive with.

Josh grinned. "Your wish is my command."

"If only," she muttered under her breath. But he heard.

His grin grew wider.

"SexyDude" turned out to be the email name used by George Hammond. Hammond, a rather nondescript, stoop-shouldered man with a seriously receding hair-line, worked as a tax form preparer for one of the larger tax consultant firms. They found him with a client and extracted him in order to have "a few words" with him.

Bewildered, Hammond became rather hostile when he realized he was being questioned about the way he'd spent his previous evening. He became even more so when Diana Kellogg's name was brought up.

"I'll tell you how I spent my evening with her," he said angrily. "I didn't. She never showed. I went to that expensive club she picked out—they had a damn cover charge," he complained. "I sat there for two hours, nursing one watered-down drink and watching the door, waiting for her to walk in. But she never showed up." A little of his anger subsided as he looked from one detective to the other. "Why are you asking me about her? Has she done something?" He seemed almost eager to hear something bad in connection with the woman who had stepped on his ego.

"No, not intentionally," Bridget replied solemnly.

"Then what?" Hammond demanded.

"Diana Kellogg was murdered last night," Josh told him. Both he and Bridget watched the man's face.

"Murdered?" Hammond echoed incredulously. Then, rather than display any sense of horror or outrage that someone should wantonly snuff out a life like this, Hammond actually seemed to be smiling. "Well, I guess that if she was murdered, she wasn't really standing me up."

For two cents, she would have wrung the jerk's neck, Bridget thought.

As if reading her mind, Josh placed his hand on her shoulder, anchoring her to her spot. "No, your reputation as a SexyDude is still intact," Josh told the man.

George looked pleased by that.

Idiot! "We might be in touch," Bridget told him. "Don't leave town."

"Can't," Hammond responded, looking at her as if she was simple-minded. "We're heading into my busy season."

"He wasn't affected by her death at all, just relieved that she hadn't actually stood him up. What a jerk." She glanced at Josh as they walked out of the building that housed Hammond's company. "Did you get it?" she asked.

Josh held up his cell phone. It was set to "camera mode." "Got his chinless profile right here," he assured her.

She nodded. "Let's go back and show it to the bartender."

"If he can tear his eyes away from you long enough to look at it," Josh commented.

"You can convince him," she said, giving his shoulder a pat.

Chapter 8

"You guys again?"

It was obvious that the dark-haired bartender at The Hideaway was less than thrilled to see Josh and Bridget making their way over to the bar, especially since it was now during the club's core hours of operation.

"I can see why you have so much repeat business here, what with that winning, outgoing personality of yours and all," Josh commented as they reached the bar. "Excuse us," he said pointedly to two of the patrons as he elbowed them out of the way so that he and Bridget could get closer to the bartender.

"Don't recall you bringing any business the first time around," Raul retorted.

"Now, Raul, play nice," Bridget advised, offering the man a big, bright smile. "We just want to see if you recognize someone." She glanced toward her partner. "Show him the picture, Josh."

Annoyed, Raul reminded her, "I already told you, she wasn't—" And then he curtailed his protest as he saw that the photo on Josh's cell phone wasn't of the dead woman he'd already disavowed. Squinting, Raul took a closer look, then nodded. "Yeah, him I saw."

Straightening, he pointed over to a table on the far side of the bar. "He sat at one of the side tables, holding on to the same damn glass of beer for like two or three hours. He was staring at the door the entire time, like he was expecting someone really fantastic to come through. Could have heard the nerd sighing all the way over here each time the door opened and whoever walked in wasn't who he was waiting for."

"*Did* anyone come over to him?" Josh asked him.

"Nope." Raul shook his head to underscore his point. "It was obvious right away that he'd been stood up. He started to creep out some of the regulars, sitting and staring like that. I was going to go over to talk to him, tell him to go home, when he saved me the trouble. He just got up and left all of a sudden."

"Do you recall what time that was?" Bridget asked, mentally crossing her fingers.

Taking an order from one of the people at the bar, Raul picked up a colorful bottle and poured the drink, then pushed the glass toward the patron.

"I think about eleven," he finally answered. "Why? Does it make a difference?"

She uncrossed her fingers. "Yeah, it makes a difference. It gives him an alibi," Bridget answered, trying to hide her disappointment. She'd really thought they'd found Diana's killer. She should have realized that would have been too easy. With a nod, she stepped away from the bar. "Thanks for your help."

Raul's attention was already elsewhere as orders came flying at him from along the crowded bar.

"He could be lying," Josh told her as they wove their way over to the front door.

"Why would he?" she asked.

Josh laughed shortly and shrugged. Taking out his keys, he pointed them toward the vehicle. "I haven't worked that part out yet."

"There might not be anything *to* work out," she pointed out.

As the car's security system was disarmed, she heard the locks popping up. Bridget opened the passenger door and dropped into her seat. It felt as if all the energy had been temporarily drained out of her.

"We're back to square one, aren't we?" she murmured, dejected.

"Looks that way—unless one of the other detectives came up with the name of a likely candidate from that stack of academy washouts they were going through when we left."

And that, they both knew, would be an exceptionally tall order. Despite the fact that it had been her idea, Bridget didn't hold out much hope that there was anything to be found there.

"It's got to be someone who looks good for all the murders," Bridget reminded him.

She sighed again. Right now, she was feeling pretty damn hopeless about being able to find *anything* worthwhile.

Josh took his cue from the tone of her voice. "It's

getting late. What d'you say we knock off for the night and get an early start in the morning?"

That seemed to snap her out of it, despite the fact that, just for a second, it did sound tempting.

"I say no," she answered flatly. "I mean, you can do whatever you want to, but I'm going back to the squad room."

Damn but the woman could be stubborn. "And what?" he asked. "Beat your head against the bulletin board?"

Maybe he didn't get how determined she was to bring down this psychopath. "If I thought it would help, yeah. But since it probably won't, I thought maybe I'd go back to the first case. This investigation wasn't ours back then," she reminded Josh. Two other detectives had been on the case the first year. One of them had become so frustrated, he'd taken early retirement several months later.

"Maybe we reviewed it too fast," she went on, "missed something the first time around. We were too focused on the latest murders at the time to do justice to number one. Number one would have been where all the mistakes were made," she said, thinking out loud. "The one that was the original crime of passion."

Josh mulled over what she'd said. "If it really was number one."

Did he know something that she didn't? Bridget wondered. "What do you mean?"

Josh was working out his theory as he went along. "Maybe the Lady Killer hid his first murder for exactly the reasons you just mentioned. After he got even with the woman for standing him up, or ditching him, or maybe even not noticing him—whatever he thought her sin was—he discovered, quite by accident, that he *liked* killing. He realized that he got off on the power of it all or maybe it made him feel like some kind of king of the world, or, better yet, a god."

The more he talked, the more he felt his theory was plausible. His voice took on conviction as he continued.

"Whatever the reason, our killer had to have his fix again. Especially when February rolled around. The month just made him feel too miserable, too hopeless and he needed to find a way to crawl out of that hole. His way turned out to be killing his 'lost love' again. And again." Finished, he studied Bridget's face to gauge her reaction and if she agreed. "Is any of this making any sense to you?"

"Yes, actually it does," she admitted. "You realize this means that we're going to have to start digging through old, *unsolved* homicides." She emphasized the word "unsolved" because if the case had been solved, the serial killer wouldn't still be out there.

The proposition sounded daunting, but she didn't see any way around it. Otherwise, they had nothing to work with.

New theory or not, Josh still thought it was a good idea if they went home tonight. "How about I buy you dinner, then we call it a night and come back fresh in the morning?" he suggested. "You look dead on your feet, Bridget," he observed. "Falling asleep at your desk isn't going to help solve this thing."

She wanted at least to get started tonight. That wouldn't happen if Josh didn't start the car, she thought, impatiently. "I'd work on my flattering skills if I were you or you definitely will have trouble landing a woman once this thing is behind us."

"Don't worry about me 'landing a woman,'" Josh told her. "Never had any trouble yet." He inserted his key into the ignition, then left it for a moment as he continued talking. "Besides, in a pinch, I can always turn to you for some female companionship."

He couldn't have surprised her more if he'd tried. "Me?"

He grinned at the look on her face. In a way, he found the trace of innocent surprise enticing. "Yeah, last I checked, you were a female, right?"

Her eyes narrowed. "Just how closely did you check?" she asked.

"I've got eyes, Detective. And you've got a figure that would really look bad on a guy," he informed her, deliberately sounding matter-of-fact. "So, what sounds good to you?"

He did, Bridget found herself thinking. "I don't know," she responded, then added in a whisper as she looked at him, "surprise me."

They had been in and out of the car countless times in the last two days, spending most of them in close proximity, not to mention close quarters whenever they were on the road in the vehicle. As she uttered her last words to him, Josh realized that having her so close stirred him in ways that surprised him. He wasn't quite prepared to deal with it.

His resistance was, admittedly, drastically low. Plus that damn scent she was wearing had been haunting him all day.

That was what he ultimately blamed for what he did next. He wasn't being himself. But whoever he was, he discovered in the seconds that followed that he was *really* enjoying himself in a way he'd never believed possible.

At least, heaven knew, not with Bridget.

Instead of starting up the vehicle and driving to one of the myriad take-out places that catered to those caught up in Aurora's fast pace, he leaned in toward Bridget, framed her face between his hands and kissed her.

And stopped time.

Half a heartbeat before his lips came down on hers, she was about to ask him what the hell he thought he was doing. But then he was doing it and there was no real reason to ask because she *knew* what he thought he was doing.

Unless he'd suddenly been possessed by an alien life form, Joshua Youngblood knew *exactly* what he was doing—and so did she.

He was curling her toes. Not to mention curling other stray body parts as well, including all ten fingers of her hands.

It was a lucky thing she was curling them, Bridget thought, because it kept her from lacing her hands around his neck. That would make it look as if she were compliant with what was happening. She really didn't want him to think that.

Even if it were true.

She wasn't sure she was ready to admit that to him. Or even to herself.

She *would* admit that she now saw what the noise was all about when it came to Josh. And she understood why Josh could get away with being such a player without having been shot yet. A woman could probably forget and forgive a great deal if she thought she might be on the receiving end of this amazing experience again sometime in the near future.

God, but it felt good. *Really* good.

It was becoming harder and harder for her not to thread her arms around his neck, despite the emergency brake that separated them.

She definitely felt as if she were on fire and about to go up in smoke. What's more, she didn't care.

Josh couldn't have really explained what had come over him just then, or what had prompted him to kiss his partner at this particular junction of their working day.

But now that he was doing it, he was glad. Glad that his resistance was down and his thinking had abruptly taken a holiday. Otherwise, he would have never discovered that the woman he'd been partnered with for the last three years, the woman with whom he had shared thoughts and body armor, and to whom, he had to admit, he felt closer than he did to any other human being on the face of the earth, had the ability to fry his brain.

Fried or not, Josh knew one thing to be true. Bridget Cavelli, aka Cavanaugh, was hot. She was also a woman of substance. Who would have thought it?

The desire to deepen the kiss and take it to the next level urgently, insistently, clawed at him, grew stronger by the moment. Any second now, he was certain, it would get to unmanageable proportions and this was neither the time nor the place to allow that.

This should go at a slower pace. He'd just willingly stepped out onto a minefield and one misstep would rend him into tiny smithereens.

He needed to pull back.

No matter how much he didn't want to.

Bridget struggled between desire and a sense that Josh was suddenly drawing away. The world, listing badly on its axis, was only gradually righting itself and coming back into focus.

She blinked, staring at Josh, wondering if she'd somehow slipped into another reality via an invisible vortex. She had no other plausible explanation for what had just happened—or for her reaction to it.

"Surprise," Josh finally said in a soft voice.

He'd drawn away, but not far enough so that she couldn't feel the warmth of his breath. Goose bumps popped up in response.

He was grinning that lopsided grin of his, the one that simultaneously annoyed and enticed her.

"What?" she bit off breathlessly. She decided that her best recourse here was to act as if she was angry and offended despite the fact that she was neither.

"You said to surprise you," he reminded her.

The words she'd uttered an eternity ago, before the world had tipped over, came back to her. Doubling her fist, Bridget took the opportunity to punch him in the shoulder, hard.

"Idiot!" she bit off. "I was talking about food."

His eyes dipped down to look intently at her lips. "Some might say that was food for the soul."

She raised her chin, looking as if she was ready to go fifteen rounds with him, after which she fully expected to be declared the winner. "And some might say that you've just gone off your nut."

For a second, Josh inclined his head, as if agreeing with her. But then he said, "And others might say that it was the smartest thing I'd ever done." His eyes held hers for a second. There was only a trace of humor on his lips. "I had no idea you could kiss like that, Bridget."

The inside of her mouth had gone inexplicably dry. If it had been up to her to spit on a fire to put it out, the fire would have raged out of control. It took effort not to allow her words to stick to the roof of her mouth.

"The subject never came up," she finally replied. Deftly changing the topic before she fell headlong into it—or grabbed him so that he would kiss her again— she abruptly said, "Chinese."

"Chinese?"

"Yes, Chinese. I pick Chinese," she told him impatiently. "Food," she added when he gave no indication that he understood where she was coming from. "Chinese food. Unless you've changed your mind and decided to skip dinner."

"Well," he allowed, squelching the urge to run his thumb along her very alluring lower lip, "some might say that I've already had dessert so maybe I'd better backtrack and have some dinner now," he said philosophically.

She glanced at him, then looked away. "If you know what's good for you."

Bridget was casting her vote on the side of putting all this behind them and just going on as if nothing had happened. But they both knew that you couldn't un-open the floodgates once they'd been raised and the waters were rushing at you.

"Trouble is," Josh said as he finally started up the car, "I think I do."

It was all he said and for once, he didn't elaborate, leaving Bridget to try to figure out if that meant that he wanted to kiss her again, or felt it was safer and more prudent not to.

Had Josh kissed her because of some silent challenge he had issued to himself—or because he actually really wanted to?

Bridget was undecided as to which side she was rooting for. Both were problematic for different reasons So, for now, she pushed the whole incident—fleeting by most standards—behind her.

Or tried to.

"Anything?" Bridget called out to the three detectives they were working with as she and Josh walked into the squad room.

Just about on their way out, the three detectives on loan, Cox, Langford and Kennedy, stopped and looked at what Bridget and Josh had just brought in. Especially Josh, who balanced various white bags in a large cardboard box. Between the two of them there had to be eight white bags, all embossed with the logo of The Sun Dragon, a red dragon exhaling a wall of fire. It was an agreed-upon fact that The Sun Dragon was the best restaurant around Aurora, possibly the county, for Chinese food.

"Is that to bribe us to stay?" Joel Langford, the youngest of the three, asked.

"Well, there's no overtime pay authorized—*yet,*" she emphasized with conviction, sure that once the cases were reviewed—and solved—there would be. "So we thought we could at least feed you. You have to eat, right? And you have to be sitting somewhere while you eat, right? So why not here? And if you continue glancing through the files, what's the harm? A lot of people read while they eat," she said innocently.

Cox exchanged looks with the other two detectives. No one appeared taken in by her innocent expression, but the food did smell tempting.

"When she says it, it sounds so logical," Cox told the other two men. He was already shedding his jacket and putting it on the back of his chair again.

"When you've been around her as long as I have," Josh told the others, "you learn not to waste your breath arguing with Cavanaugh. There's no winning against her so you might as well just say yes, shut up and sit down. Save yourself a lot of grief that way." He placed the bags in a central location and proceeded to take the large containers out of each one.

Kennedy laughed, following Cox's example and making himself comfortable again.

"You sound more like a husband than a partner," he told Josh.

"God forbid." Josh laughed, pulling up a chair.

And that is something you have to remember, Bridget told herself as Josh's words echoed in her head. The man might stir the blood, but he simply wasn't the kind to stick around. Ever. She'd seen him go through enough girlfriends in the last three years to fill up a medium-size theater. No matter what, Josh put his philosophy into play every single time.

The problem was, she could still taste him on her lips. It made her thinking process a little fuzzy.

Determined to erase all physical traces of Josh from her lips, she went for the shrimp in lobster sauce first, relying on the fact that there were always a lot of onions, as well as garlic, in the mix.

That, and a little amnesia, should do the trick, she thought. Or at least she hoped so.

Chapter 9

The Lady Killer's first known victim, a twenty-five-year-old redhead named Phyllis Jones, came complete with a distraught fiancé who, according to Detective McGee's notes in the file, had an alibi for the time of her murder. And while Bridget hated the thought of dredging up her murder again for the man if he actually was innocent, they still needed to interview the man to see if he had alibis for the time of the two most recent murders.

If he didn't, they'd take it from there.

It still wasn't an interview she was particularly looking forward to.

"I'll go with you," Josh volunteered when she announced where she was going and why.

"You don't have to," she told him. "God knows

there's enough work here to keep you busy even if you worked at warp speed—which you don't."

"Yeah, I do 'have to,'" he said stubbornly. "On the outside chance that you turn out to be right," he added.

Pulling her jacket from the back of her chair, Bridget stopped and looked at him. "Are you telling me that you don't think I can take care of myself?"

The edge in her voice did not go unnoticed. "You?" he laughed. "Hell, if you're right, I'm going along to protect the 'suspect.' Given the way you feel about these murders, you're liable to put a bullet between his eyes just as soon as bring him in."

She squared her shoulders as she gave Josh a frosty glance. "I can control myself," she informed him. Her eyes narrowed. "You're the one who can't." With that, she turned on her heel and walked out of the squad room.

"Uh-huh." The word might have indicated he agreed with what she'd just said, but there was very little conviction in it.

For now, Bridget gave up and let him come along. Two opinions were always better than one.

Ryan Roberts, a freelance architect and the first victim's fiancé, was home, working, when they rang his bell forty minutes later. He opened the door a crack, an uncertain expression on his face until Bridget held up her identification. Absently, she noted that was the first time she'd used her new ID since she'd had the name on it changed.

"Detectives Youngblood and Cavanaugh. We're with the Aurora Police Department's homicide division," she told Roberts, putting her wallet back after a beat.

Still wary, Roberts opened the door and stepped back. "Why are you here?" And then he answered his own question with another question. "Did you find him?" he asked, looking from one detective to the other. "Did you find the bastard who killed my Phyllis?"

"No, I'm afraid not," Josh answered with more compassion than he usually employed, Bridget noted.

"Then I don't understand." Average in height and slight in build, the man became reticent again. "Why are you here?"

"We just needed to ask you a few more questions, Mr. Roberts," Bridget told him, slipping into her friendliest tone to put him at his ease.

It didn't work. There was still a look of suspicion on Roberts's face. "I already told the other detectives everything I knew three years ago. They'd grilled me over and over again like they thought I was the one who did it, wasting all that time instead of going after the real killer."

Josh moved in a little closer to the man. "You sound as if you know who that was."

"I don't know his name," Roberts admitted, "but I know what he looks like."

Bridget exchanged looks with Josh. This was something new. There was no mention of another man in the file they had gone over. "How do you know that?" Bridget asked.

"I know because the little creep kept following her around, trying to talk to her, to get her to pay attention to him." A flash of anger was in his dark green eyes. "Phyllis was nice to everyone. Too nice. I guess because she did talk to him, he thought she was interested. He asked her out and she told him that she couldn't go out with him. That she was already engaged to me. He called her a liar, that he didn't see any ring." There was a tortured expression on Ryan's face when he told them, "I was saving up for one. I wanted it to be special, like she was."

A ragged sigh broke free from his lips. After all this time, Roberts was apparently still beating himself up. "I should have given her a cheap one until I could have afforded better. He would have never bothered her if he'd seen the ring. It's my fault she's dead."

Moved, Bridget put her hand on his shoulder. "It is *not* your fault," she insisted. "This man is sick. Chances are he would have still stalked Phyllis and killed her anyway."

A weak attempt at a grateful smile came and went from his lips. "I guess we'll never know, will we?"

"Would you happen to know if this guy asked Phyllis out on Valentine's Day?" Josh asked.

Ryan cocked his head slightly, thinking. "Yeah, he did. That was the day."

"And she never mentioned his name?" Josh pressed, hoping that Roberts might remember a chance reference to the other man.

Roberts shook his head. "No. She just referred to him as 'that sad little man.'"

Josh tried another approach that might lead them to a few answers. "How did she meet him?"

Roberts was silent for a moment. It was obvious he was trying to remember. "I think she said he came into her store—she managed a pet shop that specialized in food for exotic pets. He told her that he had a pet cockatiel that was sickly. He kept coming back with more

questions, most likely just so that he could talk to her."
Roberts's voice trailed off.

This was definitely a possible suspect worth looking into, Bridget thought. "Would you mind if we got
you together with a sketch artist?" she proposed. "See
if we can come up with a picture of this guy?"

"I'll do you one better than that," Roberts countered.
He walked over to the large, tilted desk he had set up
in the living room where he did all his work. "Give me
a few minutes and I'll sketch this guy for you myself."

"That would be great," Bridget told him. She saw the
look on Josh's face and immediately knew what he was
thinking. This was beginning to feel a little too easy.
Maybe Josh had a point. "Oh, by the way, since he was
stalking your fiancée, when did you get a chance to see
this guy? I would have thought that someone like him
would avoid any kind of confrontations with other men."

Roberts explained without a second's hesitation. "I
looked out my window and saw him hanging around
the corner. When I mentioned it to Phyllis she looked
out the window and said that was her not-so-secret ad-
mirer. I wanted to call 911 or at least go down and tell
him to get lost, but she said not to. That he was harmless. I should have realized people like that were never
harmless."

"Like I said, not your fault," Bridget assured him
with conviction. "Now if you don't mind doing that
sketch for us, we'll be out of your hair," she promised.

"Right away," Roberts said. He sat down and started
to sketch.

"You do realize that this looks like every second guy
in the neighborhood," Josh said to her, referring to the

sketch he was holding in his hand as they went back to their vehicle.

"Still, it's something to go on. Cases have been solved on less." Reaching the car, she took a second look at the drawing. It *was* rather unremarkable, she thought. Taking the drawing from Josh, she placed it in the folder on her seat. "Maybe if we show it at that pet shop, one of the employees might recall having seen him. Maybe the guy bought something there and used his credit card."

"Ever the optimist," Josh said.

"Hey," she protested as she got in, "optimists are right sometimes."

Josh buckled up before putting his key in the ignition. "Do you find it a little odd that there was no drawing in the first victim's file?"

"Luke McGee was a really impatient man. Half the time he didn't hear what you were saying because he was busy working out a theory in his head." Bridget felt it only fair to give the man his due. "He was a good detective, but not exactly detail-oriented and he was definitely not the easiest man to work with. He had his own drummer that he marched to."

He looked at her, intrigued. "You sound like you speak from experience."

She shrugged. It wasn't exactly a time she liked to dwell on. "I was partnered with him for a little while." And then she decided that he deserved to know a few more details. "He was hard-nosed and could be very difficult if he wanted to be. I gave serious thought to quitting the department once or twice."

Josh grinned broadly as they drove to the next light. "But then you hit the jackpot."

She laughed at the description. "Not exactly the way I'd put it."

"That's why I said it for you," Josh told her. "I know how shy you are."

He almost laughed out loud as he said the word. If there was *ever* someone who didn't come across as shy, it was Bridget. But even as he thought it, the very word made him think of something else.

"By the way, you are going to that gathering on Saturday, aren't you?" he asked.

For a minute, she'd almost forgotten about that. As much as she was into family, she was still working all of this out in her head, trying to reconcile herself with the fact that her family had suddenly quadrupled.

"Why?" she asked. "Are you volunteering to take my place?"

He grinned, turning left at the light. "I think they'd notice the difference."

"With all those Cavanaughs milling around? They wouldn't even know that I wasn't there," she assured him.

Josh was quiet for a moment, as if he was mulling over what she'd just said. Or perhaps how she had said it.

"You need backup?" he asked her out of the blue.

Bridget laughed. The idea of needing backup attending a so-called family gathering sounded comical, but then, as she turned the thought over in her head, it began to sound more than a little appealing. "Are you trolling for a family?"

"Just kind of curious to watch you in action with yours," he admitted. He thought of what she'd said was the reason for having this party. "Besides, it might be interesting to meet the man who's responsible for this whole 'Cavanaugh dynasty' that's sprung up in the police department. All those policemen who kept visiting my mom and me after my father died were all great guys—and they were almost like family. But the operative word here is 'almost.' It might be interesting to see the real thing."

He'd always struck her as being footloose and fancy-free, not someone who would welcome family ties. Maybe she should reevaluate her view of Youngblood.

"Are you looking to 'borrow' my grandfather?" she asked him, amused.

"I'll let you know once I meet the man and get to know him a little," he answered vaguely. "Besides, you seem less than thrilled about attending. I figure you might feel better about going if someone was in your corner."

She looked at his profile as he continued to drive. That was really thoughtful on his part. He kept surprising her lately. Especially the other day.

She reined in her thoughts, refusing to dwell on what had happened. It would only make her want an encore and that, she instinctively knew, would be a very bad idea.

"I guess you really can be a decent guy every so often," she commented.

His eyes on the road, Josh grinned at her flippant assessment. "It does happen occasionally, but not enough to ruin my reputation," he assured her. "So, what time do you want me to pick you up?"

"You really want to go to this thing, don't you?"

"Andrew Cavanaugh sets a fine table," he reminded her. "I've been to a few of the Christmas parties he throws for everyone. Going with you to this little get-together, I get to eat a great meal and make sure you don't get overwhelmed with all that family. It's a win-win situation as far as I can see."

Although she had to admit, if only to herself, that she did like his company, she didn't like the fact that he thought she might need moral support. It didn't matter that she might, she still didn't like him thinking it. It made her seem vulnerable.

"I don't need a keeper, Youngblood," she informed him.

He took her defensiveness in stride. "How about a friend? Or do you not need one of those, either?" he asked.

He'd found just the right way to get to her. There was no point in protesting any longer. "Two o'clock," she answered, shifting so that she was looking straight ahead rather than at him.

"Two o'clock it is."

She could hear the satisfaction in his voice. "Now can we get back to work?"

"We never stopped," he told her cheerfully.

Without her realizing it, they had arrived at the precinct. Josh pulled up into their spot in the parking lot. Shutting off the engine, he glanced at the folder where she'd tucked in the sketch. She'd mentioned showing it around the place where the first victim had worked, but now he thought of other places as well.

"You know, it might not be a bad idea to show that around to the other victims' relatives or friends, see if any of them remember seeing this guy lurking around somewhere."

She had been thinking the same thing. It amazed her

how in tune they could be sometimes. Bridget nodded. "Worth a shot. Meanwhile, maybe we can have this run through a facial recognition program."

"Better yet, how about the database with the DMV photos?" Josh suggested. "Just the ones from Northern California." Getting out of the vehicle, Bridget took out the sketch. Josh tapped it for emphasis. "I mean, this guy's got to have a driver's license, right? He doesn't ride the bus to the scene of the crime and he doesn't use the bus to transport the bodies."

What Josh said triggered a thought in her head. "Not unless he's a bus driver and uses the bus after hours for his own purposes every so often."

Josh stared at her, amazed at how she kept coming up with these theories. "You've got an answer for everything, don't you?"

She shrugged. "I think we need to look at this thing from all different angles," she told him. "Something's bound to click eventually."

"In the meantime, it can also make you crazy," he pointed out.

"I can't argue with that," she said as they walked up the stairs to the back entrance.

"Sure you can," he assured her with conviction. "You could argue with God about whether or not the sun comes up in the east."

Oddly enough, the comment didn't bother her. Being viewed in that light was a lot better than being thought of as vulnerable.

Once in the building, rather than reporting to Howard the way the lieutenant had insisted they do each time they returned, Bridget and Josh brought Roberts's sketch to Brenda.

They found the woman still busy working with the last victim's laptop.

"What are you looking for?" Bridget asked, puzzled. "You already found the guy from the internet dating site's IP address."

"Yes, but I also found something else," Brenda answered rather proudly. "Totally by accident," she admitted. She waited for a moment, as if to build up the suspense, before telling them that "Somebody hacked into her laptop."

"You mean like someone was trying to steal her identity?" Josh asked Brenda.

"No." Which made it all the more interesting. "From what I can see, this person hacked into her computer so he or she could read her email."

Bridget's mouth dropped open. That was it. That was how the killer knew where to find her. "If he read her email, he'd know that she was meeting the internet dating guy at The Hideaway—and that's why Diana never showed up for her date."

Josh nodded in agreement, picking up the thread. "He could have been waiting just outside the club, identified himself to Diana as her date—remember, she didn't know what the guy was supposed to look like— and say that he knew a better place for them to go."

Brenda was listening to both of them as they talked faster and faster. Raising her hand, she cut into their rhythm. When they both looked at her, waiting, she asked, "Wouldn't that make her suspicious?"

Josh had already thought of that. "Not if he gave her a good reason why he decided that some other club—or restaurant—might be better. Work with me here," Josh urged the women. "This was how he got her to come with him. He knew all about her—"

"Not to mention that she looked just like his first victim," Bridget interjected. The photographs on the bulletin board she'd set up in the squad room had an eerie sameness to them, as if the women could have all belonged to the same family.

"Which he would have known from that social network page," Josh said, looking at Brenda. "Any way to find out if this guy looked at anyone else who looked like our victims?"

"Maybe in a parallel universe, but it's not anything that I can do," Brenda said.

"Can you find the IP address of the hacker?" Bridget asked.

"It's definitely not going to be easy," Brenda warned her. She looked back at the laptop screen uncertainly. "Whoever this guy is, he's really good."

"Yeah, but so are you," Josh told the woman. The smile on his lips was warm and encouraging.

"Flattery will get you somewhere every time," Brenda told him with a laugh. She knew exactly what he was doing, but she also knew what she was capable of if she pushed hard enough. "But when Dax complains that he hasn't seen me in a week, I'm sending him over to you so *you* can explain why I haven't been home."

Josh grinned. "Leave it to me. You track down the hacker for me and I'll personally send the two of you on an all-expenses-paid second honeymoon."

Brenda glanced up, humor glinting in her eyes. "What makes you think we're done with our first one?"

That, Bridget thought as they left the lab a couple of minutes later, was the kind of marriage she wanted. One where the love didn't wear out once the newness of the situation faded away.

But even as she thought it, despite everything she knew about the way Josh operated, she couldn't help glancing at him.

And wondering.

What if...?

Chapter 10

"You clean up good," Josh said when Bridget finally opened the front door.

It was Saturday and two o'clock, the time she'd told him to come by. He'd been all but leaning on her doorbell since she didn't answer the first two times he'd pressed it. When at last the door *did* open, he'd meant to say a few sarcastic things about her taking her sweet time.

But those words completely evaporated in the heat generated of his partner in a gray-blue dress.

The long-sleeved dress only came midway down her thighs, but it lovingly adhered to every curve of her body during that journey even when she wasn't moving.

Josh made the comment to her in self-defense, hoping that the semi-flippant assessment would annoy her enough to draw attention away from the fact that he'd been momentarily stunned into silence by her appearance and had all but swallowed his tongue.

Granted, since he'd already given in once and kissed her, he'd suspected that Bridget was a great deal hotter than their day-to-day relationship would have normally made him believe. But in his wildest dreams, Josh wouldn't have expected that she could look *this* hot.

"You make it sound as if I come in to work looking like something that the cat wouldn't drag in on a bet," Bridget said.

The comical description made him laugh. With a careless shrug he conceded, "Well, maybe not quite that bad."

"But bad?" she pressed incredulously. "You actually think I look bad when I come into work?" She always tried to appear professional and at her best when she came into the squad room in the morning.

"You fishing for a compliment, Cavanaugh?" he asked, raising one probing eyebrow. He made no attempt to hide his amusement. "Okay, I guess I can give you a compliment. You're an attractive woman, partner, we both know that. But to be honest, I really had no idea that you were this hot."

She did her best not to allow a superior, satisfied smile curve the corners of her mouth. No doubt he'd probably have a crack about that, most likely something about her wanting to appeal to him. God forbid he got started on that line of thinking, even though, secretly, his reaction did please her—maybe a little more than it should have.

Even so, she just couldn't pass up the opportunity to make a quip.

"Maybe your radar isn't as good as you think it is,

Youngblood." She tilted her head as she pretended to study him. "Ever think of maybe having it overhauled and updated?"

He'd never really noticed how brilliantly blue her eyes were. Or just how very female she could be.

Or maybe he had, he reasoned, and had gone out of his way to pretend that he hadn't, just like he was trying to block the scent of her perfume now. You couldn't have distracting thoughts about your partner and still operate at maximum efficiency.

But right now, neither one of them was on duty and he was noticing a hell of a lot of things he shouldn't be. Like how enticing her breasts were as they rose and fell with each breath she took.

If he wasn't careful, she'd damn well take *his* breath away.

"Right now," he told her seriously, his voice low, "you wouldn't want to know what I was thinking."

Warning bells went off in Bridget's head. There were a lot of layers to his words and she was wise enough to step back.

"If you've changed your mind about going," she told him, "I can drive myself over."

"I never said that," he pointed out. Seeing her looking like this, Josh wanted to go to the family gathering more than ever. He put his hand on the doorknob. "Ready?" he asked.

Bridget's eyes met his. Something strong undulated through her. If she had an ounce of sense, she'd head straight for the hills.

She didn't.

"Ready," she answered.

He doubted that either one of them really were ready.

* * *

"You're just in time," Brian declared warmly as he opened the front door to admit them. Andrew had asked his younger brother to man the door while he put the finishing touches on something in the kitchen. "The old man just arrived about five minutes ago. He came in the back way and hasn't been out to address everyone yet," the chief told them. He ushered the two of them through the foyer. "Get yourselves a good space to stand in," he advised. "As I recall, my dad could talk the ears off a statue once he got going."

She looked at Josh. "Last chance to back out," she whispered.

But Josh shook his head. "You're not getting rid of me that easily. My ears are glued on tight." Placing his hand to the small of her back, he ushered Bridget into the living room.

As he did, he glanced around. It astounded Josh just how many members of the police department were scattered through the ground floor of the former chief of police's spacious house. It was a matter of record that the Cavanaughs' numbers were not exactly minor. Looking at them now, with their spouses and children around them, Josh found the number to be all but staggering.

Thinking of the precinct, he asked, "Anyone minding the store?" bending close to Bridget's ear so that she could hear him above the not inconsiderable din.

Bridget struggled not to shiver as his breath cascaded down the side of her neck, making it hard to catch her breath.

It took even longer to find her voice. "I'm sure

there're one or two police officers left to defend the good citizens of Aurora."

"I wouldn't count on it," Josh said. He accepted a glass of wine from a woman carrying several on a serving tray. She seemed vaguely familiar. "Thanks," he acknowledged, then finished his sentence. "I see a few non-Cavanaughs here, too. It looks like the whole police department is here."

"Non-Cavanaughs?" she repeated. "You mean like besides you?" Bridget shook her head when the woman—Andrew's daughter, Teri—offered her a glass of wine as well.

"Yeah," he answered. The whole house teemed with police personnel now that he looked closer. Maybe there *wasn't* anyone left patrolling the streets. "You know, if I was an enterprising crook, this would seem like the perfect time to knock off a string of gas stations in Aurora."

Teri Cavanaugh-Hawkins couldn't help overhearing. She didn't bother trying not to laugh. "You call that enterprising?"

"He's had a tough week," Bridget told the woman with a grin. "Cut him some slack."

Teri's eyes danced and she paused, studying Bridget's face. It was obvious that she was trying to remember the other woman's name. "You're… Kendra?" Teri asked, catching her lower lip between her teeth.

"I'm Bridget," Bridget corrected. "Kendra's older sister." Although the difference was only a matter of thirteen months, as children it had been this insurmountable chasm and she'd rubbed Kendra's face in it.

"Sorry." Teri flashed an engaging smile, then promised, "I'll get it right next time."

Josh took a sip of his wine. "You Cavanaughs should come with flash cards," he commented. "At the precinct is one thing." For some reason, he was accustomed to seeing the various members of the clan there and could distinguish between them despite the strong resemblances. "But en masse and in civilian clothes, hell, that's a whole other story."

"Don't worry." Frank, one of the chief's stepsons, came up behind Bridget and Josh and placed a hand on each of their shoulders. "There's not going to be a quiz at the end of the evening."

Zac, Frank's older brother, came in from their other side and joined the growing group. "However, there will be one when you want to get into the precinct come Monday morning. How's it going, Youngblood?" he asked gregariously, picking up a drink from the near empty tray Teri was holding. He and Josh had worked together a couple of times in the past. "Our newest cousin drag you here for the big meet-and-greet?"

"I did not drag him," Bridget protested. "He insisted on tagging along."

"What was the draw?" her older brother, Thomas, asked as he too joined the group. On his arm was a tall, slender, stunning redhead, who was also his fiancée. Kaitlyn Two Feathers, the newest detective to permanently join the department, was a recent transplant from New Mexico. Thomas looked from his sister to the buffet against the far wall. "You or the food?"

"The food," both she and Josh answered at the same time. The grin on her brother's face, Bridget noted, was smug, as if he'd expected them to answer in unison for some reason. She knew better than to question Tom with so many people around. She might hear what she didn't want spread around. So, for now, she ignored both his grin and him.

Instead, she turned to Zac and asked, "Do you know where the chief's father is?"

"You mean our grandfather?" Tom prompted.

It really felt strange hearing someone being referred to as their grandfather, Bridget thought. By the time she was four years old, neither the people her father believed to be his parents, nor her mother's parents, were alive. The idea of having a grandparent was an entirely new sensation for her.

"Yes," she answered. "Our grandfather." She looked toward the chief's stepsons for an answer.

But it was Teri who pointed the man out to her. "He's right over there," she said. "With Dad and Uncle Brian."

Flanked by two of his sons, Andrew and Brian, Seamus Cavanaugh looked more like their older brother than their father. Six feet tall with wide shoulders and a trim waist, his once-jet-black hair was as thick as ever, but it had turned a gunmetal gray. Despite that, his features were still startlingly youthful.

Bridget decided that it was the man's wide smile that made him look younger than his seventy-three years.

It was another several moments before she became aware of the fact that the older man wasn't just walking into the center of the room, he was walking toward someone.

Toward her father.

A large lump came out of nowhere, rising to her throat as she watched Seamus Cavanaugh embrace the son he had inadvertently been separated from almost five decades ago.

Everyone around them burst into spontaneous applause, touched to be part of this reunion, which was to some a miracle in its own right.

Seamus cleared his throat as a host of emotions, led foremost by joy and wrapped tightly in disbelief, fought to gain control over him.

"You look just like your mother," he managed to tell Sean. Then, in a vain attempt to hold back his tears, Seamus said, "I guess you're too big to take for a pony ride."

Laughter erupted after the observation. The family patriarch was referring to something that had become a tradition for him. As each of his sons became old enough, he would take the boy to have his picture taken sitting astride a pony and wearing Western clothes right down to a pair of stitched boots and a cowboy hat.

Brian had copies of the individual pictures on his desk and Andrew had them on the wall of his den. There were three. One of Andrew, one of Brian and one of Mike, the brother who had died in the line of duty. There had never been a fourth one because the brother they believed to be Sean had never lived to see his first birthday. The pictures reflected Seamus's weakness for Westerns.

As the laughter continued, Seamus held his hand up for silence. When it came, he looked around at the members of his family who were gathered around him and observed, "There were a lot less of you when I left."

Smiling, he slowly scanned the area. The faces he remembered had grown older. And there were new faces, some belonging to children who had been born while he was living on the other side of the continent, others belonging to spouses his grandchildren had exchanged vows with.

He'd missed a lot, Seamus thought.

"Maybe I should have come back sooner." Seamus paused for another moment, his steel-gray eyes sweeping over the very crowded room, then coming again to rest on his newfound son. "They say as you get older, life stops surprising you." The corners of his mouth curved again. "They lied."

His heart swelled. Seamus put a strong, firm hand on Sean's shoulder, remembering. And regretting.

"I only wish your mother was still alive so I could tell her that I was sorry and that she was right. She would have loved that." Realizing that some might not understand what he was referring to, he explained, "She swore that the baby we brought home from the hospital wasn't the baby she'd given birth to. I thought she was just stressed out from the ordeal. You were a really *big* baby," he told Sean.

A wave of laughter met his comment.

"I should have never doubted her. Mothers always know," he gladly admitted.

Seamus took in a deep breath and it was obvious that he was struggling to steady his voice and to suppress the emotions threatening to break free.

"We have a lot of catching up to do, you and I, son." He put his arm around Sean's shoulders. "What say we get started?"

"I say great," Sean responded, his deep, resonant voice choked with emotion like his father's.

And for the second time in her life, Bridget saw her father shed tears. But, unlike when her mother died, this time the tears were happy ones.

Tears like her own, Bridget realized belatedly as the dampness on her cheeks registered with her consciousness. She sniffed, doing her best not to draw any attention to herself or the tears she subtly wiped away with her hand.

And then a handkerchief was being silently pressed into her hands. Not by any of her newly discovered relatives, or her brother, who was standing on her other side. To her surprise, the handkerchief came from Josh.

What surprised her most of all was that Josh gave it to her without uttering a single word or comment. Her partner usually teased her about her being emotional, or soft, or something along those lines. Her warmth for Josh grew. The man could really shock her.

Clutching the handkerchief, she wiped her eyes. A moment later, more tears gathered, seeking immediate release. She wouldn't have thought she could get so emotional.

It was obviously a day for surprises.

During the course of the evening, she and her brothers and sisters, as well as Tom's fiancée, were all introduced by their father to their grandfather.

The older man, like his sons Andrew and Brian, had an uncanny ability to make each person feel singled-out and special while he spoke to them. The man really meant it when he said that he wanted to spend time getting to know each one of them. She believed him when he told her that he intended to be a hands-on grandparent from now on.

Andrew, however, eyed his father skeptically. "What about Florida?" he asked.

Sitting on the wide sofa, surrounded by his new grandchildren, Seamus looked over to his firstborn. "What about Florida?"

Andrew had thought, when his father had called to

say that he was finally coming back to Aurora, that he meant on a visit. No mention had been made of staying indefinitely.

"Well, for one thing, your house is there," Andrew pointed out.

Seamus surprised more than a few people who were listening when he shook his shaggy head and told them, "Not anymore. I put the house up for sale." He looked around at dynasty that he had given birth to, marveling at the miracle of it all. "You might as well know, I'm moving back here."

"Back here?" Brian repeated. "But I thought you loved living in Florida, being retired. You called it living the good life."

"Turned out not to be so good," Seamus answered, then elaborated. "A man can only take so much sitting around, doing nothing." He thumped his chest with a closed fist. "I'm still alive so it's high time I started acting that way."

Brian glanced over toward Andrew, who moved his wide shoulders up and then down in a mystified shrug. Neither of them had a clue where their father thought he was going with this.

Brian was the first to put it into words. "Just what does that mean, Dad?"

"It means," Seamus began, then paused impishly for a moment as his gaze swept over the faces of those sitting closest to him, "that Seamus Cavanaugh's getting back in the game."

Andrew and Brian exchanged looks again, this time a little uneasily. That was the way their father had always referred to police work. No one wanted to hurt the old man's feelings, but he had to face the fact that he was just that: an old man.

"Dad," Andrew broached tactfully, "you're a little over the age limit to be talking about rejoining the police department."

"You mean too old," Seamus said bluntly. "Well, in case you haven't noticed, I'm also too old to be taking orders from some wet-behind-the-ears kid young enough to be my grandson—or granddaughter," he tactfully included, nodding toward several of his grandchildren. "Which is why I'm opening up my own detective agency," he announced, ending on a note of fanfare as he gleefully rubbed his hands together.

He let the news sink in before continuing, "And Andrew, if you ever decide you've had enough of standing over a hot stove, feeding this bunch…" He chuckled. "You might think about coming to work for me—or with me," he corrected. Seamus raised his hands and then spread them out wide, as of tracing a large, imaginary sign. "Cavanaugh & Cavanaugh." His eyes twinkled as he looked around the room. "It has a nice ring to it, doesn't it?" Seamus asked with a wide, pleased smile.

"It's official," Bridget heard someone behind her say. "Grandpa's back."

That, too, she couldn't help thinking, had a nice ring to it.

Apparently, Seamus heard the comment from one of his grandchildren. "You bet I'm back," he answered. "And I intend to make up for lost time."

"Take it slow, Dad," Andrew advised.

"Slow?" Seamus's hearty, infectious laugh filled the air. "Are you kidding? I can't take it slow. It's not like I've got another forty years to work with this time around," he reminded his son. "Slow is for young guys like you," he told Andrew. "Whatever I do, I've got to do fast."

"Don't burn yourself out, Dad," Rose, Andrew's wife, warned her father-in-law. "You're going to live to be a hundred."

It was obvious that the older man was pleased by the prediction. "Well, then," he allowed, "I'm going to wind up packing a lot of living into those twenty-seven years," he predicted.

No one in the room doubted it. Not even those who hadn't known the man before today. They were all in agreement that Seamus Cavanaugh was a force of nature and a dynamo, determined to reclaim his place in the world. No one doubted that he would, too.

Chapter 11

"Now that's what I call a family," Josh said, laughing softly to himself.

It was eleven-thirty and while the party was still going on at Andrew's house as they had left, it had grown smaller and consequently more subdued in nature. Approximately half the people who had attended had already said their good-nights and drifted out the door, making their way toward the cars parked along the next two blocks.

Josh had made no indication that he'd wanted to leave. Instead, he left that up to Bridget, waiting for her sign that she was tired or thought that it was time to go. Initially, even though he'd sensed this afternoon that she'd been rather reluctant to come at first, as the evening had worn on, he began to get completely opposite vibrations. It was obvious that his partner was enjoying herself, enjoying watching her father get to know the man who was *his* father.

Eventually, though, Josh noticed her stifling yawns and then, finally, she caught his eye and nodded. Over the course of the last three years, they had developed a sort of shorthand. It was time to go home.

Tired himself, Josh lost no time in taking her at her word. Making the rounds in double time, he and Bridget said their goodbyes. He had her out and in his car in a little more than two heartbeats.

Leaning back against her seat, Bridget laughed in response to his comment now. The Cavanaughs en masse were definitely a force of nature.

"And here I thought I came from a large family." Until this evening, when every single family member had made it a point to show up, she hadn't realized just how huge the family actually was.

Josh slanted a look in her direction, a smile playing on his lips. "You do."

She knew what he meant. Josh was referring to the "small town" they had just left behind them. But thinking of all of them as family would take some getting used to on her part. Yes, they were Cavanaughs and yes, apparently she was, too, but actually *feeling* like one of them would take adjustment.

"No, I'm talking about my core family," she stressed. "My dad, my brothers and my sisters. There's eight of us altogether, counting Dad, and I always thought that was a lot."

He thought back to their entrance and how overwhelming it was to see that her family was taking up every available inch of space in the house. "Not when you compare them to the Cavanaughs."

That was what she was trying to tell him. "My point exactly."

"Still," he went on, mulling the situation over in his head, "it must be nice, knowing that they're there to support you and that they have your back so completely. *Nobody* will mess with you now that you're a Cavanaugh. I hear it's all for one and one for all with that clan."

"I wouldn't go that far yet," she told him. "I mean, they barely know me."

Josh didn't see the problem or why she was hesitating. If it were him, if he had suddenly discovered that he was related to the Cavanaughs, he would have already declared it to the world and opted for a family portrait. Having a family, people with a vested interest in you, appealed to him immensely.

"What's to know? You're a Cavanaugh. That's good enough for them," he assured her. "I never saw a more united bunch of people. It's as if they were all tuned in to one mind."

A smile she couldn't quite fathom played on her partner's lips as he continued talking. Was it wistfulness? Envy?

"Makes me realize what I've missed." Josh said the last words more to himself than to her.

If it was family he wanted, she had more than enough to spare—not to mention that there were times when she would have gladly paid someone to take her brothers off her hands. Things were much better now, but there was a time…

"I've got a few spare brothers I could lend you," she offered. "All slightly used, but they still have a lot of mileage left on them. Just say the word and they're yours."

Turning a corner, Josh laughed and shook his head. "Not that I'm not grateful, partner, but it's not quite the same thing."

Her brothers could still be pretty irritating at times, especially when they thought they were right and she wasn't.

"Trust me, Youngblood, a little while with any of them and you'll be very happy that you're an only child," she promised him.

She sounded sincere, but he had only one question for her. "Would you want to be a loner if you had the chance?"

A flippant answer rose to her lips, but then Bridget saw that he was really serious. If she was going to be honest with him, there was only one answer she could give him.

"No, I wouldn't," she admitted. Because she had a large family, there was always someone to talk to, someone to turn to if she needed a soundboard or a shoulder to cry on. Having a family as large as hers had ultimately given her a great sense of security, a feeling of being safe no matter what.

She wouldn't have traded her life with anyone else's for the world.

Bridget's prolonged silence gave him his answer. "I didn't think so." Her apartment complex was the next right and he took it. "Both of my parents were only children. If my dad had lived, I know they would have had more kids. My mother told me she wanted at least three." Lost in his thoughts, he pulled up into an empty space in the guest parking area. But even as he turned off the ignition, he remained sitting in the car. "After hearing that, I always tried to be three times the son she could have asked for," he confessed with a disparaging laugh. "And probably three times the headache."

Getting out of the vehicle, Bridget pretended to try to envision that. "Wow, three of you would be more than anyone should be forced to put up with," she told him with an exaggerated shiver. "How did your poor mother survive that?"

Josh automatically walked her to her door. "Very funny," he commented.

Coming to her door, Bridget fished out her key and then turned around to face her partner. All things considered, he was a pretty good guy. They were together a minimum of eight hours a day and yet he had volunteered to accompany her to this party, sensing that she needed to have someone with her, a warm body who was on her side. She couldn't deny that she really did appreciate his doing that for her.

"Thanks for having my back, Josh," she said softly, as if saying the words louder would make it seem all too serious.

Her comment caught him by surprise. After a moment, Josh shrugged. "It's not exactly as if we were pinned down at a shoot-out and you were caught in the cross fire," he pointed out.

"Yeah, but I was kind of—uneasy about it." Bridget was going to say "nervous," but that would have been too much of an admission on her part. "I really do appreciate you coming with me."

Josh grinned. "You mean inviting myself along."

Bridget inclined her head and grinned back. "I was trying not to be blunt."

In his experience, his partner had never been what someone might term a shrinking violet. "Blunt" had probably been her middle name at one time or another. "Now that's a first."

Here was the Josh she knew. She was more comfortable reacting to his sarcastic, flippant remarks than to his random act of kindness. The latter put her at a disadvantage.

"You know what? Never mind." She waved her hand at him, dismissing her partner. "Subtleties are wasted on you."

Very slowly, Josh allowed his eyes to drift up and down the length of her, taking in the way her dress still highlighted far more than it hid. Her body was tight, firm, and his knees, he noted, were beginning to feel just a wee bit weak.

"Oh, I don't know about that," he contradicted.

Bridget did her best to ignore her reaction to his languid scrutiny. "You could at least look me in the eyes when you say that."

Josh flashed a full-on sensual grin. The expression in his eyes made her gut tighten twice over. "Not that your eyes aren't pretty, but who knows when I'll get a chance to see you looking like this again?"

Not in a hundred years, she silently vowed. He made her feel vulnerable and that wasn't good. "Careful, your libido is showing."

The grin on his lips only deepened, creating more ripples inside of her. Josh shook his head. "And I was trying so hard to hide it."

If she didn't know any better, she would have said that Youngblood was flirting with her. "What's the matter, Josh, no new woman in your life?"

He watched her for a long, pregnant moment before finally saying, "Not in the usual sense, no."

He'd moved closer, Bridget realized. Somehow, as they stood there, bantering, exchanging words, the air had grown warmer and the distance between them had grown a lot shorter.

Or at least it certainly felt that way.

Her throat went very dry. She swallowed, but it didn't help.

"Then in what sense?" she challenged.

Only when the words were out did she realize that she'd whispered them. She really hoped that he wouldn't notice, but she had a sinking feeling she didn't really have a prayer.

He needed to get going, Josh told himself. To turn on his heel and leave right now before he did something stupid. Something he'd wanted to do since the moment she'd opened the door this afternoon.

It was all very simple, really. He knew how to walk. How to put one foot in front of the other and create space between himself and whatever it was that he was leaving behind.

And yet, there he was. Standing still.

Not moving.

And then he was. But he wasn't moving in the direction he needed to go. Instead, he was moving to close the tiny bit of space that still existed between him and Bridget. Moving until that sliver of space was completely blotted out. Until there wasn't enough space between them for the thinnest sheet of paper to fit in.

The only way she would save herself was through bravado and she knew it.

"You're in my space, Youngblood," Bridget informed him hoarsely, trying to sound annoyed.

"What are you going to do about it?" he asked, well

aware that this could go either way. The way he wanted it to or the way he didn't.

In all honesty, he half expected his feisty partner to place her hands on his chest and shove him back. Hard. The one thing he hadn't expected—admittedly longed for, yes, but really wasn't expecting—was to have Bridget grab hold of the sides of his jacket, raise herself up on her toes and press her mouth urgently against his.

And just before she did, he could have sworn that she'd whispered, "Damn you!"

But he wasn't able to ask her why, because by then her mouth was on his, creating such havoc inside him that all he could think of was kissing her back with the same intensity.

He wanted to rock her foundations the way she was rocking his.

Bridget's heart pounded wildly even as the most remote part of her brain, the part that hadn't been fried to a crisp yet, demanded to know what the hell she was thinking, kissing him at all, let alone like it was the end of the world.

But the simple truth of it was, she wasn't thinking. She was going with gut feelings, with demanding sensations. With a hunger that she would have sworn she wasn't even vaguely acquainted with.

Except that now she was.

Josh had triggered something within her, feeding an untamable hunger inside.

In a velvet haze, Bridget was feeling around along the door behind her, searching for the keyhole. Finding it, she fitted her key into the lock in what could only be the most awkward angle ever assumed by a human being. But she was desperate to get inside her apartment, desperate to drag Josh in with her, and insanely determined not to lose even a moment's contact with him.

Somehow, she managed to unlock the door and get it open.

The next second, they were stumbling inside, lips still very much sealed to one another even as articles of clothing began to fly off.

She felt constricted by what she was wearing, bound, imprisoned. She needed to shed every last stitch so that she could satisfy this overwhelming need to feel Josh against her.

Feel his hands, his torso, his desire.

So even as she shed her spectacular dress as well as its accessories, leaving articles discarded in a tangled, forgotten heap, she was yanking at his clothing as well. She was gratified as she felt him shaking free of his jacket, pulling away his shirt and then stepping out of his jeans, kicking everything aside so that the path was clear for them.

His body was hot as it pressed against hers.

As hot as his mouth, which was no longer sealed to hers but roaming along her throat, her shoulders, her neck, creating chaos and wild, thunderous desire with each pass that he made.

It was a night of revelations.

Just as she was convinced she'd reached the pinnacle of pulsating desire, he managed somehow to bring her up yet another notch.

Caught up in this tango they were dancing, a silent tango composed of throbbing rhythms she could feel within her body, Bridget suddenly stumbled, tripping backward. His arms immediately closed tightly around her, but instead of breaking her fall, Josh went down with her.

Down and twisting so that when they reached the floor a split second later, Bridget found herself on top of him.

The feel of his hardened body excited her, bringing her up to such a high plateau that she could scarcely catch her breath. And all the while, her heart pounded as his mouth continued to roam over the length of her. She could feel herself quivering against him.

Under oath Josh wouldn't have been able to say just how this had come about or what had come over him. Yes, he'd been attracted to Bridget for a long time now and yes, he'd spent the evening keenly aware of her proximity, her scent, her very existence. But he'd always maintained control over himself, known how to keep both his temper and his desires in check under all circumstances.

So what had happened here?

How had this slip of a woman—a strong woman, granted, but still not his match in height and weight by any means—how had she managed to bring him down to his knees, destroying every last shred of his self-control while she was at it?

All Josh could think of was how much he wanted her. How much he needed her.

Desired her.

He knew deep down in his gut that if he didn't try to fill himself with her, he would cease to exist. Cease to be.

It was an absurd thought.

And yet, somehow he knew that it was true. That

if he was to continue living a moment longer on this earth, it would take having her, making love with her, to sustain him.

The fact that Bridget didn't attempt to resist, that she not only welcomed him but had been the one to instigate this crazed, fateful dance, only managed to urge him on further and more quickly.

He'd never kissed anyone who kissed him back with such ardor, such passion before. Never wanted anyone with such intense longing. It was more than a fever of the blood, it was bordering on insanity and as much as he absolutely hated the fact that he was being held prisoner by these feelings, that he had absolutely no free will when it came to his fate, he couldn't seem to break free.

And after a few timeless minutes had faded from existence, he didn't want to.

Didn't want to be free of her or of this need for her. What he wanted, more than life itself—which truthfully scared him to no end—was to have her. To take her now and make her his alone.

Now.

No matter what the consequences.

With one calculated movement, he had Bridget under him.

Balancing his weight on his elbows and knees, the rest of his body so close to hers that boundaries between their two bodies were difficult to define, he framed her face with his hands.

"Look at me," he ordered hoarsely, desire constricting his very throat. When she didn't comply at first, he repeated the instruction more firmly, waiting for her to do it.

Drawing in a shaky breath, Bridget opened her eyes and met his.

There was no anger, no defiance, not even a look of submission in her eyes. Just challenge and desire. She felt the way he did.

It was all he needed to know.

With his eyes on hers Josh drove himself into her, making her his.

Making himself hers.

And then it began, the scrambling journey to the top, to take hold of the wondrous sensation that occurred when all inhibitions disappeared and two, however briefly, became one.

His arms tightened around her and he had to hold himself in check not to cause her any undue pain as the final moment swept them both breathlessly away.

Chapter 12

For several minutes there, as they lay on the floor side by side, Bridget was fairly convinced that she would never catch her breath again, that she would never move normally. Her heart beat so hard that she felt too weak even to get up, much less to walk and talk.

What had he done to her?

What had she *allowed* him to do to her?

Too exhausted to move, Bridget continued to lie there, with the back of her wrist pressed against her eyes, warding off not just the light streaming into her apartment through the kitchen window, courtesy of the full moon, but hopefully the immediate world as well.

Her dazed, chaotic mind searched madly for something coherent for her to say, *anything* that would sound neutral and innocuous so he wouldn't know just how very deeply he'd shaken up her world.

Finally, desperate to bring an end to the silence and the sound of her own irregular breathing, Bridget muttered something, in hindsight, that she considered incredibly inane.

"I didn't turn on the lights."

"Yeah, you did," she heard Josh say. Even without looking at him, she could "hear" the grin on his lips.

What the hell was he talking about? They'd all but fallen into the apartment, never once bothering to turn on any of the lights. At this point, she considered it lucky that they'd closed the door. Passion had completely knocked out any common sense that might have been lying around.

Confused, she lifted her wrist and opened her eyes to glance at him.

"You turned on a whole spectrum of lights," he told her, then lightly tapped the center of his chest with his fisted hand. "Right in here. There were starbursts and even a mesmerizing light show."

Was this actually Josh talking to her like this? Admitting to being moved? Or was he setting her up for some big payoff? Or maybe some big joke?

For as long as she'd known him, Josh had never bragged about his conquests, only about having stellar evenings—or entire weekends—and he'd always end his quick summation with a sensuous, amused grin.

But he never gave her any details—not that she'd ever asked.

She had to admit that she liked that about him, that he kept things like that and what went on behind closed doors between him and his myriad lady friends to himself. It told her that somewhere along the line, someone had made an effort to see that Josh grew up to be a gentleman.

A gentleman who could make the earth move.

Turning her head to look at Josh, and getting an extremely queasy feeling in her stomach as she did so—a good queasy feeling, she thought with an inward smile—Bridget asked, "Should I be checking your garage for a pod?"

"Don't have a garage," he told her, almost drawling. "Have a carport." Like her, he lived in a garden apartment complex.

"Any pod left there would have been moved by the rental office," she speculated, giddy and still far too tired to attempt to move.

And then she became aware that Josh had raised himself up on his elbow and was looking at her. Suddenly, she wasn't so tired anymore. Feeling around on the floor, she searched for an article of clothing, *any* article of clothing larger than a handkerchief so that she could cover herself.

But there was nothing there except for the rug. Frustrated, she reached over her head and pulled down the seat cushion from the sofa and placed that on her body. It balanced precariously.

"Looking for a floatation device?" Josh asked, amused. "I don't think the weather bureau predicted any flash flooding for the area." He found her modesty almost sweet. And rather futile. Very gently, he tugged away the cushion. "You realize that's like locking the barn door after the proverbial horses have run off."

He was right, of course, but that didn't keep her from being stubborn. "It's my barn door," Bridget argued. "I can do with it whatever I want."

"That it is," he agreed. "And you can." And then his smile turned from amused to sensual. "All I ask for is squatter's rights."

Bridget could feel warmth spreading throughout her entire body. The kind of warmth that promised to turn her a bright, bright shade of pink from her head to her toes. And he noticed the progression starting.

"Hey, Cavanaugh," he said, calling attention to the color her skin was turning. "You're blushing."

"No, I'm not," she bit off.

He was going to make her pay for this occasion of weakness, wasn't he? This was a mistake, a damn mistake. Why hadn't she stopped herself while she still had a chance?

Because she'd wanted it too much. And now she was going to pay for it, Bridget thought, trying to resign herself to her fate.

"Okay," he allowed, "then you must be lying on something very hot because you're turning a shade of pink I've only seen on preteens and salmon steaks while they're being grilled. The salmon, not the preteens," he added with a widening grin.

He was laughing at her, she thought angrily. Sitting up, Bridget scanned the immediate area, looking for her dress. Why hadn't she been more careful when she'd done her frenzied striptease and taken note where she'd dropped her clothes?

Suddenly spotting her dress, Bridget made a dive for it.

Unfortunately, she had to turn her back on Josh to do it and he found that the view succeeded in arousing him all over again. His partner, he thought not for the first time, was one fine-looking woman.

"If you don't want to turn me on, Cavanaugh, I suggest you find yourself a blanket and wrap yourself up in it *now*." He stressed the last word, conveying a sense of urgency to her. He wasn't about to take advantage of her, but what he did want to do was to seduce her into doing what they'd just done all over again.

Holding the dress, rather than slipping it on and having it reveal more than it hid—since she had no undergarments on—Bridget held it up against her as she turned around again to look at him.

"You're telling me I'm turning you on?" she asked incredulously. The Josh she knew would have *never* admitted to something like that. It completely went against his love-'em-and-leave-'em facade. Just who *was* this man she'd just made love with?

"Right now, Cavanaugh, you could turn on a rock. A petrified rock."

She didn't want him to see how much his words affected her. She wasn't nearly as experienced as he was—who was?—but she wasn't exactly a babe in the woods, either. The last thing she wanted was to hear Josh gloating that she'd been moved by his compliment. She did her best to appear unaffected and blasé.

"Does that line usually work for you?" she asked him, a smirk on her lips.

"Work for me?" he repeated as if he didn't quite follow her.

"Does it get you 'repeat business'?" she stressed. When he still didn't seem to get it, she elaborated even further. "The women you make love with, does saying that line to them have them suddenly desperate to do it all over again?"

"It's not words that they're after," he told her evenly, his meaning clear.

He was telling her the reason the sexual partners he'd had were so eager to make love with him again was because of his technique, not his words. He really had made the earth move, but she would die before ever telling him that.

His eyes seemed full of sensual mischief as he tugged her back down to him. "So, how about those 49ers?" he teased, referring to the San Francisco football team.

"You'll have to ask Logan," she said, bringing up the name of one of her brothers. "He's the resident expert on football."

The sensual smile still very present on his lips, Josh ran his fingertips over her mouth. "And what are you an expert on?"

"I haven't picked an area of expertise yet. When I do, I'll let you know."

Her eyes fluttered shut almost involuntarily as she felt Josh sensually brush his lips—just the slightest point of contact—against her shoulder. Even that fleeting touch sent goose bumps racing up and down her spine.

"I really wish you wouldn't do that, Youngblood," Bridget said. It took effort to squeeze the words out evenly.

He drew his head back a little, as if studying her. "Nope, you don't mean that," he told her simply.

Her back went up. No, she didn't mean that, but he was being just a little too cocky for her taste. "Why? Because you're so damned irresistible?"

Lucky for her he liked feisty women, Josh thought.

The more she resisted, the more she aroused and interested him.

"No," he told her very simply. "Because you're crinkling your nose. You always crinkle your nose when you're lying. It's your 'tell.'"

"You studied my face?" she asked in disbelief, stunned.

"Among other interesting parts," he said, unable to resist giving her a leer. "I like knowing my partner inside and out."

She just bet he did. Bridget raised her chin defiantly. "There's such a thing as too much information, you know."

"Maybe." His smile went straight into her nervous system, causing an instant upheaval. "But not in this case."

Leaning down over her, Josh kissed her. Not passionately the way he had in response to her first kiss earlier, but with small, soft kisses landing gently on her lips like the first spring butterfly delicately perching on a rose petal just before it flew off.

If possible, this had an even greater effect on her than his passionate kiss had. She could feel her very core igniting as desire galloped through her even *more* urgently than the first time. Surrendering, giving up all resistance to this man, she reached for him.

The next moment, he had her in his arms and was abandoning any thought of reining in his feelings. They had this moment and he intended to enjoy it—enjoy her—with every fiber of his being.

Who knew what tomorrow might bring?

Amid the passion and the ardor, the sound of first

one cell phone ringing, then two, took a little time to penetrate.

Bridget wanted nothing more than to ignore it and just absorb the wild feelings shooting through her. But she knew she couldn't pretend her phone wasn't ringing. She was a detective with the Aurora Police Department and that meant that unless she was lying on a table in the operating room and was actively under the knife, she was expected to be on call anytime, anyplace. No matter what.

As was Josh.

Drawing her head back, she looked up at him. His phone was ringing as well.

Resigned, she reluctantly reached for her cell phone. It took her a moment to focus—and then she realized what the call had to be about.

Oh God, please not again.

"Cavanaugh," she declared grimly a second after she unlocked her phone. Her voice blended with Josh's as he announced, "Youngblood."

They were both on the phone and both looking at each other, dreading confirmation that the Lady Killer had struck again.

"He's out of control," the voice on the other end—Langford—told her. Frustration echoed in his deep voice. "The Lady Killer just killed victim number three and it's not even the tenth yet."

"Where?" she asked, sitting up and dragging her hand through her hair. As the detective on the other end of the line spoke, she scanned the room, trying to locate the rest of her clothes. Listening to Langford she was also attempting to make out what Josh was saying at the same time.

He wasn't saying much, but his face had grown grim. "Be right there," he told the detective who'd called him. "No, I've already left the chief's party," he replied to Kennedy's question just before he shut his phone and terminated the call.

There was no reason to state the obvious. The Lady Killer had upped his ante and was on a spree.

"At this rate, he's going to double the number of his total kills by the time he gets to the end of the month," Josh said grimly, standing up.

Bridget suddenly found herself caught in two very different worlds. In one, she was the consummate detective, her mind on the case, in a hurry to get herself together so she could get to the scene of the crime as quickly as possible.

In the other world, she was a woman who'd just been utterly blown away by her partner and was, even now, while in the midst of a tragedy, utterly captivated by Josh. The latter had just stood up, as unencumbered by clothing as the day he was born and completely unself-conscious about the figure he cast.

He had one hell of a magnificent, taut body, she couldn't help admiring. Even her fingertips were tingling.

"Maybe you should get dressed a little faster," she suggested, her throat feeling just the slightest bit tight.

Picking up his clothes from the floor, Josh looked at her quizzically. "Why?"

"Just do it," she snapped, turning her back on him and marching off to her bedroom.

She didn't see Josh grinning at her.

If she was going to be up all night—and this had all the earmarks of an all-nighter—she might as well be comfortable. Going to her closet, she pulled out a pair of jeans and a pale blue turtleneck sweater. She moved quickly, got dressed and hurried out, a pair of boots in her hand.

Almost dressed, Josh was buttoning up his shirt. She sat on the edge of the sofa, pulling on her boots. He gave her a quick once-over.

"Oddly enough, you look just as sexy in that as in the dress you had on tonight. Of course, that might have something to do with the fact that I know what you look like naked," he added with a smoldering, lethal grin.

Glorious as it had been, it was a mistake and she knew it. Most workplace affairs fizzled out quickly, leaving behind a residue of awkwardness if not worse. If that happened, ultimately they would wind up getting different partners, which was a shame because whatever else went on between them, she and Josh worked extremely well together.

"I'd rather you kept that to yourself," Bridget told him.

Finished buttoning, he tucked in his shirt and then held up his hands.

"No problem," he said. "I wasn't exactly planning on posting it on YouTube."

He was staring at her, she noted. Again. Braced for some kind of punch line or snappy comment at her expense, she told herself she might as well get it over with. "Okay, what?"

"Nothing," he answered noncommittally. "It's just that you think you know a person after interacting with them on a daily basis for over three years and yet there always seems to be some kind of surprise just underneath the surface."

She had always liked surprises. "I would think that's a good thing."

"Didn't say it wasn't," he replied in his laid-back manner. The same sort of pseudo-country-boy manner that drove her crazy.

Their phones rang again and they exchanged looks. Bridget had a sinking feeling in her stomach.

"Oh God, don't tell me there's another one besides the one they just called about," she groaned. That seemed incredibly macabre, even for the Lady Killer.

"Only one way to find out," Josh said, pulling his phone out of his pocket. "Youngblood." She could have sworn she saw him square his shoulders and snap to attention a beat before he said, "Yes, Chief. No, I wasn't asleep yet."

Her phone began ringing. Why was the chief of detectives calling him, she wondered even as she opened her own phone. This seemed a little beneath the man's level of operation.

"Cavanaugh."

"So, I'm glad to hear you're finally using it," the deep male voice on the other end told her with resonant approval.

"Chief?" she asked uncertainly, looking at Josh. Why was the man they'd left at the party calling both of them on a conference call? Was the man checking on them for some reason?

Had he suspected the way the evening had gone and called to confirm?

Brian Cavanaugh didn't strike her as the type to pass judgment on the personal lives of his people, but then, she wouldn't have guessed that Josh was as good as he was—or as thoughtful—either. Her ability to read people had been temporarily suspended.

"Yes, it's me, Bridget. I've got you both on conference call," Brian told the duo. "Thought it might save a little time that way. I take it the two of you are in the same area."

She took a breath, then said, "Yes, sir," wondering if this was just an innocent question on the chief's part or if, as she feared, the man was putting two and two together. And if he did, would there be a reprimand along with some sort of consequences?

"Okay, then I'll expect to see you both here ASAP. We need to put an end to this. *Now,*" Brian emphasized grimly.

"If the chief's involved," Josh said to her as she terminated the call and closed her cell phone, "that means he's getting a lot of pressure to make an arrest and have a suspect arraigned for this killing spree."

She nodded in agreement. "Certainly looks that way. The chief of D's considers Aurora his city to personally protect." Bridget sighed, shaking her head. "Now all we need is a suspect to arrest," she muttered as they dressed and went over to the front door.

"Yeah," he agreed, setting his jaw grimly. "That would be rather nice, wouldn't it? Well, maybe this time the son of a bitch made a mistake and we can finally latch onto something. C'mon, let's go," he urged, leading the way out.

Locking her door, Bridget hurried to the waiting vehicle.

Chapter 13

She could hear herself breathe.

Josh wasn't saying anything. He hadn't said a single word to her since they'd gotten into the car. It wasn't like him.

One of them had to bring it up before it became the elephant riding in the unmarked car, taking up all the available space, sucking up all the oxygen and growing at a prodigious rate.

If he wasn't going to do it, it was up to her.

"So, what was that back at my place?" Bridget finally asked without any sort of preamble. The silence had gotten just too overbearing and unwieldy for her to tolerate.

"Pretty terrific, I thought," Josh answered with feeling. Sparing her a quick look, he added, "You were good, too."

His breezy tone, as well as the way he'd phrased his answer, told her all she needed to know about how he regarded what had happened between them.

She should have known, Bridget chided herself. What had she expected, anyway? That one encounter with her and he'd magically transform into someone who'd hang around longer than the life expectancy of a fruit fly?

"So, it was just a hookup," she concluded quietly, setting her jaw hard.

It was on the tip of Josh's tongue to confirm her assumption. To say something light and flippant, the way he always did, and to act as if, now that they were back in their clothes, it was just business as usual between them.

But it *wasn't* business as usual. What had happened between Bridget and him earlier had been different. *Really* different. And he knew damn well that he stood the chance of losing something exceedingly special if he fell back on his usual carefree, man-about-town act.

Taking a breath, Josh stepped out on the ledge and then dove off.

"Actually, no, it wasn't 'just a hookup' and I think you already know that," he added quietly.

No, she didn't. If she was being honest with herself, she'd have to admit that she'd hoped, but she really *hadn't* known. Not when it came to Josh, who went through women the way her mother used to go through tissues while watching *An Affair to Remember* for the umpteenth time.

A warm sunspot opened up inside of her. She did her best not to grin like an idiot. "So, what do you want to do?" she asked Josh.

"Truthfully?" He really had only one thought in his head. "Make love to you until I literally come apart at the seams."

It was a real struggle to keep her grin from surfacing. She knew if she came across as eager in any manner, shape or form, Josh would be gone so fast he would make the Road Runner look slow.

So, putting herself in Josh's shoes, she said, "As enticing as that sounds, why don't we take it one step at a time?"

In every other case, that would have worked fine for him. The suggestion would have been right up his alley. It didn't nail down anything, didn't promise anything. No strings, no commitments, which was just the way he liked it.

The operative word here, he realized, was *liked.* As in past tense.

He had never felt uncertain before, never been in this position before. The emotional uneasiness, even if he didn't show it, was a new sensation for him and he didn't much like it.

But to say so would be to lose face. Moreover, it would tell Bridget that when it came to this—whatever "this" that was between them was—she was in the driver's seat and his pride wouldn't allow that.

So instead, he said, "Works for me," and then turned his attention back to what had called them out in the first place. The Lady Killer and his gruesome, growing body count.

"What the hell are we going to do to stop this son of a bitch?" he wondered out loud.

"Until we have a suspect in our sights, nothing,"

she answered, every bit as frustrated as he was. Maybe even more so.

"And once we have a suspect?" he asked. Her tone of voice seemed to indicate that she had a plan in mind after that and he was curious to hear what she was thinking.

He wasn't wrong. "Then we set a trap for him and bring him down."

He couldn't have said exactly why, but there was something about the sound of that that made him uneasy. "What kind of a trap?"

"The simple kind," she answered. "The psychopath obviously likes redheads. If we know who he is, we give him what he likes. I can become a redhead in twenty minutes."

Josh scowled. That was an utterly stupid plan. What the hell was she thinking? "You can become dead in less than that," he snapped.

She looked at him, stunned. He'd never yelled at her before. Never yelled at all to her recollection. "Why, Youngblood, is that concern I hear in your voice?" she teased.

Yes, it was concern. Even if they hadn't just shared an incredible interlude together, she would still be his partner, his friend, and there was no way he was going to let her dangle herself like live bait in front of the cold-blooded shark that was out there.

But again, to tell her that would be leaving too much of himself exposed and vulnerable. He fell back on a standard excuse. "You die, I have to fill out a mountain of paperwork, explaining to HR why I wasn't there to save you."

"The best way around that," she told him cheerfully

as they got closer to the scene of the crime, "is for you to be there like the cavalry, lurking in the shadows." She gazed at his profile. "You're good at lurking, aren't you?"

"Never tried it," he told her seriously. He had already dismissed her suggestion as ridiculous.

"'Lurking' is a little like hiding," she told him, "except more obvious."

Josh didn't want to continue going down this path, or having this discussion. And he definitely did *not* want to contemplate the thought of Bridget risking her life by putting it into the hands of some unpredictable, homicidal maniac.

"Moot point," he said, calling an end to the banter. "We don't have a suspect."

"Yet," Bridget deliberately underscored. "We don't have a suspect *yet*."

He laughed shortly, shaking his head. "You really are a Pollyanna, aren't you?"

As for him, he wasn't nearly as optimistic as his partner was. Granted the police department's record for arrests here in Aurora was better than most, but in general, a lot of killers—serial killers included—were just never caught and brought to justice. He didn't like thinking that way, but it was the simple truth and he couldn't help wondering if the same thing would happen here.

Ordinarily, Bridget bristled at being labeled a Pollyanna, but not this time. And not by him. "Well, after last night, as far as I'm concerned, hell has frozen over and the devils are ice-skating, so anything's possible."

Maybe hell *had* frozen over. In any case, Josh knew

when to leave well enough alone and this was one of those cases.

They talked about other things.

"Another dump job?" Bridget asked the ME the moment she got out of the car and approached the body.

Like the others, this victim was a redhead, probably not even twenty-one years old. Her hands were clasped together, as if in prayer, right below the gaping hole that had been left. The hole where her heart should have been.

The medical examiner, Eliza Stone, a black-eyed, black-haired young woman who had been on the job all of three months, nodded. Because the angle was awkward when it came to conducting a conversation, she rose to her feet before speaking.

"He killed her somewhere else and dumped her body here." Her mouth set grimly, she looked from one detective to the other. "This guy is definitely a professional."

"Yeah, a professional nut job," Josh said disparagingly.

"That, too," the young woman agreed. "But I wish I had his precision. He didn't make a single unnecessary cut or stroke on her skin." Eliza looked back down at the killer's handiwork. "This guy's very skillful. This sort of thing takes training."

"You're obviously not talking about him attending serial killer school." Josh's eyes narrowed. "You're not talking about a—"

"—surgeon, are you?" Bridget asked, finishing her partner's sentence for him as her eyes widened in horror and disbelief. Doctors were supposed to be the good guys, the ones who stitched you up and made you whole, not the ones who stole organs and hollowed you out like some macabre Halloween pumpkin. That just didn't make any sense.

"Actually, I guess I am," the young woman answered in dismay.

Stunned, Bridget turned toward the ME. "Why didn't you say anything about this before?"

The reasons had sounded right in her head at the time. Now, she realized the error she'd made. An error that possibly had cost at least a couple of girls—if not more—their lives.

"Because I didn't want to think that someone who had taken the oath to 'first do no harm' was doing more than just 'harming,' he was slaughtering," the ME admitted. "Besides, until this last one, I wasn't a hundred percent sure that he was a surgeon."

"But now you are?" Josh asked, wanting to pin her down.

"More than before," Eliza allowed, evasive up to the end.

Bridget stepped away from the ME and the body that was still on the ground. Away from the men from the coroner's office who were waiting for the body to be released so that they could transport it to await an autopsy.

"So we should have been looking for a surgeon instead of a police officer wannabe?" Bridget said to Josh, disheartened.

Once the lieutenant caught wind of this, he would have her head on a platter, she thought. She'd gone over his head to secure extra hands to go through the data files, looking for an academy dropout or reject who could have done this. Now, apparently, that very well could turn out to have been a waste of resources, man hours and money.

Head on a platter, big time, Bridget thought, trying to resign herself to that and the fact that the man might even suspend her without pay for this.

"Way I see it, we were covering all possible bases. It could very well have been someone flaunting his kills before the police department," Brian observed, surprising both of them as he walked up behind them.

"Instead of someone who doesn't seem to care if he's caught," Josh speculated.

"Or someone who is trying to *get* caught," Bridget countered.

The medical examiner frowned. "Why would he want to do that?"

"Because he can't stop himself. He needs someone to do it for him," Bridget said. "Someone to stop him. To stop his pain."

"His pain?" the ME echoed, dismissing the theory. She looked back at the latest victim. "Looks to me as if he's the one who's causing the pain."

"There are all kinds of pain," Bridget told the other woman. But she was looking at Josh as she said it.

Josh raised an eyebrow in a silent question, as if to get her to elaborate or explain just what she meant by that, and why she was looking at him so pointedly. But for once, Bridget pretended not to see him.

Turning away from the dead girl, Bridget felt her pocket vibrating. Someone was calling her on her cell. At this hour?

Didn't anyone sleep anymore? she wondered, taking the phone out. "Cavanaugh."

"Cavelli?" the uncertain voice on the other end of the line asked.

Was she going to have to make some kind of a public declaration of the name change? She had been hoping word of mouth would do that for her.

"Yes, it's me," she said, for a moment embracing her previous name. "Who's this?"

"Cox," the voice told her with a touch of surprise that he hadn't been instantly recognized. "When did you change your name?" he asked, momentarily side-tracked.

"Recently," Bridget bit off, then asked with a touch of impatience, "Did you call with something important or are you just updating your yearbook?"

She heard the other detective laugh. "You're going to kiss me when you hear."

At this point, curious, Josh joined her. Angling her hand a little so that the phone was positioned between them, Josh cocked his ear so that he could hear what the other detective was saying.

"We'll see," Bridget said to Cox. "I know I'll kill you if you keep playing games like this," she said in an unflappable voice. "Okay, spill it, Cox. Why are you calling us when we're in the middle of the newest crime scene?"

"Because—wait for it," he announced dramatically, then after a moment, continued, "I think I found our guy, Bridget."

She knew better than to get excited. Disappointment almost always followed. But things were becoming so intense, she couldn't help herself. Excitement pulsed through her veins.

She did her best to sound calm. "What makes you think so?"

The detective on the other end drew out each word. "Because I have found victim zero. The one the Lady Killer killed first, except we didn't know it," he clarified in case Bridget had missed that.

Bridget gripped her cell phone so hard, had it been alive it would have squealed. She exchanged looks with Josh. Almost afraid to breathe, she urged Cox to go on.

The older detective paraphrased what he'd stumbled across. "Three years ago, just before the guy's killing spree took on a more public nature, there was this medical student who was killed leaving the campus late one night. The coroner said that she'd been savagely slashed across her chest."

Now her palms were growing damp. "But her heart was still in her body, right?" Bridget guessed. Otherwise, it would have been flagged by the detectives who had initially worked the cases that first year.

"Yeah, right." Cox's voice grew more intense as he continued. "But reading the report, I got the impression that the killer ran off before he could finish what he started out doing. According to the autopsy, the student was barely dead when the campus security guard found her."

"And he checked out? The guard?" Josh wanted to know, speaking up. "They found him to be innocent?"

"Yup. Like fresh powder on a ski slope," Cox confirmed.

She needed to see that report. "Okay, we're coming in. Don't go anywhere," Bridget instructed. "We'll be right there."

Cox's laugh was hollow. "Where would I go?

This has become my home now," he grumbled good-naturedly. "My wife's probably having an affair with the plumber. We've been getting a lot of bills for repairs lately," he speculated, his voice trailing off.

"Don't let your imagination run away with you," she instructed as she terminated the call.

"You two have a lead?" Brian asked, waiting for Bridget to close her phone and slip it back into her pocket.

Bridget grinned hopefully and held up two crossed fingers over her head. "With any luck, yes. *Finally,*" she added with momentarily enthusiasm.

"Then get going," the chief urged. "I don't like this creep running free in my city a minute longer."

Coming from anyone else, the term might have sounded presumptuously possessive, but everyone on the force had come to regard the chief of detectives as a father figure. They knew that he felt that the city was his baby and that he intended to keep it as safe as he could by any means possible.

They slept easier for it.

By the time they reached the squad room, Bridget had picked up her pace and all but burst into the near-empty room.

"We're here," Bridget announced needlessly. Making a beeline for Gary Cox's desk, she asked, "What do you have?" The question came out breathlessly as she all but hovered over the detective's computer.

Cox obliged by punching several keys on his keyboard. Within moments, the case he'd called about was up on his monitor.

But as Bridget leaned in to look, the detective angled

the screen away from her, asking, "What, no bribes? You're supposed to bring bribes." He pretended to pout. "I've been stuck here since the bicentennial, the least you can do is bribe me with a latte."

"The bribes are coming. They've been held up," Josh quipped, turning the screen back so that Bridget could view it. "Now what do you have?"

"Gerald Green gave a statement to the police after they found the woman's body," the other detective recited, summarizing what he'd read. "Said they were engaged to be married. Turns out he was a medical student, too." Looking at the screen, he didn't see Bridget and Josh exchange glances. He had no way of knowing about this latest point that had been raised by the ME about the serial killer. "According to this, Green said they met in one of the classes and 'love blossomed over the cadavers.'"

Josh's jaw all but dropped. "Wow. Is he for real?" he hooted.

Cox nodded. "Apparently."

"We need to do a little follow-up on this Gerald Green guy," Bridget said, doing her best not to get carried away. They'd had leads before only to have them disintegrate right before their eyes. This could be another one of those.

But something in her gut said no, not this time.

"See if he went on to graduate from medical school and just where he is now," she continued. Looking at Josh, she couldn't help saying, "I've got a good feeling about this."

The next moment, she was patting Cox's shoulder. "Nice job, Cox," she told the man with feeling. And then, impulsively, because he'd said that what he had to show her would make her kiss him, Bridget brushed her lips against that man's cheek.

When he looked at her, stunned, his fingers tracing where her lips had just been, Bridget grinned at him. "Thanks."

Recovering, Cox said, "Don't mention it." And then, as mischief entered his dark eyes, the older detective began to ask, "What do I have to do to get you to—"

"Not tell your wife that you were about to make a lewd suggestion?" she finished, raising an eyebrow.

"Never mind," Cox murmured, waving his hand. "I'll let you know if I find anything else."

"You do that," she encouraged. "In the meantime, we need to get hold of Brenda and ask her to do a little digging for us." This she said to Josh as she took out her phone for the umpteenth time.

"My thoughts exactly," Josh agreed. "Except for one little thing. It's Sunday morning."

"She's a Cavanaugh," Bridget answered, scrolling through the list of phone numbers she'd recently input. "They have a code. She'll come in," she told him with confidence.

Being a Cavanaugh definitely had its perks, she thought as she heard the other line being picked up.

Chapter 14

"Thanks again for giving up your Sunday and coming in to help us with this," Bridget said to Brenda as she and Josh came into the computer lab.

Brenda Cavanaugh was already in the lab and working by the time they came down to the precinct's tech lab. Armed with all the information that Bridget had given her when she called, Brenda had immediately started the search for the whereabouts of Gerald Green, the first victim's fiancé.

Brenda brushed off the thanks. "No problem. Hey, it's in all our interest to get this guy off the street as soon as possible." She looked up at them for a moment. "Who's to say that this time around, the animal's going to stop carving up women at the end of the month? According to the reports, he's escalated his kills. Maybe he'll just go on with his spree as well until he runs out of redheads."

"Or gets caught," Josh interjected with a hopeful note.

Brenda smiled at the suggestion. Her fingers seemed to move almost independently, flying across the keyboard at a speed Josh found enviable. Surrounded by technology, he was still a hunt-and-peck kind of guy.

"From your lips to God's ears," Brenda murmured in response.

There was nothing more they could do here for the moment, Bridget thought. "Call me when you get something," she requested, then turned on her heel and retreated.

She and Josh hadn't even gotten halfway across the lab to the door when her cell phone began ringing. Pulling it out of her pocket, Bridget absently glanced down at the tiny screen as she opened the phone. Brenda's image appeared under *Caller ID*.

There had to be some mistake, Bridget thought as she placed the phone to her ear. Was there a glitch in her phone?

"Cavanaugh," she said uncertainly.

"Right back at you," she heard Brenda say.

Turning around to face the woman at the computer, the phone still held against her ear, Bridget looked at Brenda quizzically. Slowly, she hit End and returned the phone to her pocket.

"You're calling me?" she questioned.

Brenda looked at her innocently. "You said to call you when I had something."

"You *have* something?" Josh asked, stunned. The

woman couldn't have been here for very long. Just how fast did she work?

"I wouldn't be calling you if I didn't," Brenda said with a trace of seriousness.

Bridget shook her head in awed disbelief. "You are an amazing woman."

"So I keep telling Dax," Brenda answered with a laugh, as she pulled up the screen for them to look at. "Apparently our grieving fiancé dropped out of medical school when his girlfriend was killed. He disappeared off the grid for almost a year, then surfaced. From the tax forms I pulled up, he bounced around from one menial part-time job to another, never staying very long at any of them."

That could be someone who was heartbroken and couldn't move on emotionally—or someone who was trying not to get caught, Bridget reasoned.

"What's he doing now?" Josh wanted to know.

Brenda went to another screen. "Well, for almost the last two years, he's been working at a nonprofit medical transport service. It's underwritten by the Warner Foundation—" a charitable organization that was run by one of the state's more high-profile billionaires "—and for a nominal fee, the service provides transportation for elderly citizens who don't drive as well as for the handicapped."

"Sounds pretty selfless," Bridget commented. Maybe too selfless, she added silently. She saw the expression on Brenda's face. "I'm sensing that there's a 'but' coming."

"Could be," the other woman allowed. "From what I can see, nobody who was interviewed at the time of the student's murder could remember her actually *being* engaged. This includes her best friend and her parents."

That still didn't make the man a murderer, but it did raise the odds that he had been lying about his whereabouts the night of the murder. Bridget's interest was immediately piqued.

"Oh?"

"Anyone question this guy about where he was the night his so-called fiancée was killed—and why no one knew she *was* his fiancée?" Josh asked. Standing behind Brenda, he looked at the screen, but saw nothing there that answered his questions.

Brenda scrolled down the screen before answering him. Reading, she said, "Yes. According to this, the investigating detective did ask. He had an alibi for the time of the murder and it seems that the engagement had just happened. He told the detective that he had just asked her the day before and when she said yes, he gave her his grandmother's engagement ring."

"Let me guess," Bridget said, picking up the thread of events. "When they found the victim, she wasn't wearing an engagement ring."

Brenda nodded. "Give the lady a cigar. *And,*" she added, "there was no telltale line on her ring finger to indicate that she'd been wearing a ring. But then, if he'd just given it to her the day before, there wouldn't have been one formed yet."

"Conveniently," Josh murmured.

He had a feeling that the man had made everything up. Perhaps had even spun an elaborate fantasy for himself involving him and the girl. When she burst his bubble, he killed her for it.

"We have a picture of this grieving fiancé?" Bridget asked.

"Just his DMV photo," Brenda answered, pulling it up.

Bridget stared at the small picture. For a moment, there was this feeling that she'd seen the man before, but she couldn't nail it down. And then it came to her. "Who does that look like?" she asked Josh eagerly.

Josh took another, closer look. This time, the similarities registered. "The sketch that architect did for us of the creep who'd been stalking his fiancée."

Bridget grinned. "Bingo!" Turing toward Brenda, she requested, "Let me see the address to this transport service." When Brenda pulled it up, Bridget turned the screen toward her, then jotted the address down on her well-worn, dog-eared pad. Finished, she tore off the page and surprised Josh by holding it out to him. "Here, take Langford or Kennedy, whoever you find first, and see what the people running the transport service can tell you about our 'employee of the month.'"

Folding the address, Josh slipped it into his shirt pocket. They all but had the guy. Hanging back like this wasn't Bridget's style. She would have taken the address and run with it. After all, she was the lead on this case and he knew how much catching this guy meant to her.

"You're not coming?" he asked.

But Bridget shook her head. "In case he's currently at the service, I don't want him to see me."

And then he understood. Josh suppressed a wave of anger. He'd thought they'd put this to rest. "You're not still talking about that fool idea of yours, are you?"

Brenda stopped typing. "What fool idea?" she asked.

"Nothing," Bridget answered automatically.

For once, because he was so angry at the very idea of her risking her life, Josh didn't hold his peace and back her up the way he usually did. "She wants to dye her hair red and set herself up as bait for this bastard," he told Brenda.

It was obvious that Brenda didn't like the idea any more than he did. "Maybe you'll get enough on this guy from what his boss says to arrest him."

"And maybe not," Bridget countered. She didn't understand why everyone was so against this. It would make everything so much simpler. They needed proof, and while the sketch was helpful, it wasn't anything they could use in court. It was all circumstantial. "Having him try to add me to his collection of victims would make nailing him for these murders a sure thing."

Josh snapped at her, "It's not worth risking your life for."

The way she saw it, either she did it, or the dirtbag killed someone else. "You'd rather risk another victim's life instead?" she asked.

Josh threw up his hands. Sensing an ally in the woman behind the computer, he deferred to her. "Brenda, you talk some sense into her."

But instead of adding her voice on the side of common sense, Brenda surprised Josh by shaking her head.

"You're a Cavanaugh, all right. No doubt about it." Looking at Josh, she explained, "There's no talking to them when they get like this. They do what they want to, what they believe is right. Trust me," she told Bridget's agitated partner, "I know. Heads like rocks, the whole lot of them."

Josh's eyes narrowed as he regarded the source of his irritation. "I could tie you up," he threatened Bridget.

"We'll talk kinky later," Bridget promised. "Right now, we've got a killer to bring in."

Brenda laughed at Bridget's initial comment, then looked down at the computer screen and pretended to be engrossed in what she saw there.

"I'll let you know if I find anything else," she told them as they left.

Bridget's mind was already racing. "Okay, I'll come with you, but I'll stay in the car, out of sight."

"Good enough." He *knew* she couldn't just hang back. At least this way, he could be sure she wasn't doing something stupid. "If the guy's there," she was saying, "bring him in for questioning."

He didn't like the tone of her voice. She was leaving something unsaid. "And if he's not there?"

She gave him a serene smile. "Then maybe I'll get to find out what I look like as a redhead."

They were going around in circle. "I don't like this," he growled.

The smile faded immediately. Bridget became very serious. "I'm not asking for your permission, Youngblood," she informed him crisply. "If this guy *is* our killer, he's got to be stopped."

"No argument," he agreed. "But why do you have to be the bait?"

"Somebody has to," she said simply, "and I'm not about to ask someone else to do what I'm not willing to do myself." Bridget stopped walking just before they reached the up elevator. No one else was around as far as she could see. For a moment, she allowed herself to get personal. "Don't worry, you're not going to get rid of me that easily." The scowl remained on his face. "I can put it in writing if you'd like," she added when he made no response.

"What I'd like is for you to stop acting like some kind of superhero who thinks she's bulletproof," he said.

"Too late," she told him cheerfully. The elevator arrived and she walked in ahead of him, pressing for the squad room floor. "I'm already taking 'bends steel in her bare hands' classes."

He grabbed hold of her shoulders, then struggled not to shake her. "Damn it, Bridget, this isn't some game or a joke."

"I know that," she answered him quietly, her tone deadly serious. "I've read all the autopsy reports. Besides," she went on, allowing a hint of a smile to return as she tried to lighten the mood for him, "you'll be lurking in the shadows, remember? You won't let anything happen to me."

He only wished he had her confidence.

With the car parked inconspicuously out of the way, Bridget sat in the backseat, listening to Josh and Kennedy talk to the man who managed the transport service. The three were inside the building located several hundred feet away.

They had stopped back at the lab to pick up some equipment—tiny equipment—before heading out to interview the manager of the transport service, Gerald Green's boss. Josh was wearing the same sort of transmitter/receiver that she was, a tiny device that once inserted inside the ear could easily be missed. It allowed her to hear without being seen, just the way she wanted it.

Right now, as she listened to the manager speak, she frowned. Speaking with only a slight foreign accent, the man had nothing but glowing words of praise to say about Gerald Green.

"I wish I had five of him," the man enthused. "All our clients love him. They call to tell me that he's gentle, polite and I guess most important of all, that he listens to them when they talk. The guy's clearly a saint," he went on.

Bridget seriously debated marching into the building to ask what the manager was smoking if he didn't stop heaping all these accolades on the former medical student.

But as she listened, the manager only continued listing Green's virtues.

"He works the odd hours no one else wants, especially the night shifts, and he always returns the rigs looking even cleaner than when he first took them out." It was clear that Green had won the manager's heart with this single act of cleanliness. "I have to keep after the others to make sure they clean up the vans, but not him. Gerald's a self-starter. Why are you asking all these questions about him?" he finally asked.

There was silence for a moment as Josh searched for a way to phrase this without alerting the serial killer's possible unwitting ally.

"We're investigating a cold case," Josh explained. "Gerald Green's fiancée was murdered four years ago and some new evidence has come to light."

"Wow," the manager said, obviously stunned by the information. "I didn't know. He never said anything about having a fiancée or her being killed. But then, he doesn't talk much about himself. His attention is always on the clients he picks up and delivers. That's why he's so popular. Everyone asks for him, even when he's off duty. Like I said, wish I had five of him."

"No, you don't," Bridget muttered to herself.

"Tell me, was he on a run last night?" Josh asked.

The manager didn't even have to check his schedule. It was apparent that he'd already checked his log when he'd come in this morning.

"He was on duty, but no one called in according to the phone log. He left a note saying it was slow and that he was taking the rig to one of those do-it-yourself stalls to give the van a good once-over."

Yeah, I just bet he is, Josh thought. Out loud he asked, "Did anyone see him come back?"

"We just had the one guy on duty at night—Gerald," the manager conformed. "We usually don't get calls, unless someone wants to be taken to the E.R. They call us when it's not really a 911 type of emergency," the man explained.

"Where is Green now?" Bridget heard Kennedy ask the manager.

"He's working a double shift," the manager answered. Pulling up a screen on the office computer, he located the driver. "Said he needed the money. He went out on a run over an hour ago to pick up Mrs. Phelps on Baker Street and bring her over to her daughter's house—we do that sort of thing to pick up some extra money when it's slow," he explained.

And then, frowning slightly, the man glanced at his watch. "But he should have been back by now. We don't have the van wait for our clients. We drop them off,

then go back out and pick them up when it's time." He
looked again at his watch even though not more than
half a minute had gone by. "Don't know what could be
keeping him."

The manager laughed to himself. "Unless, of course,
he's off somewhere cleaning his van again. He's prac-
tically OCD about that," he confided to the detectives.
"Hates to see anything out of place or dirty. Takes a lot
of pride in keeping his vehicle absolutely spotless. You
could probably eat off those floors."

Or kill on them, Josh couldn't help adding silently.
"Well, you've been very helpful," he said aloud to the
manager. He and Kennedy rose to their feet. "We'd appreciate you giving us a call when Mr. Green gets in,"
Josh said. He took out one of his business cards and
placed it on the manager's desk blotter.

"Sure thing." The manager left the card in the center
of his desk. He shook his head again in wonder. "A
murdered fiancée. Who would have thought? Just
shows you how closed-mouthed the guy could be. If
it'd happened to me, I'd tell everybody. Get a little play
out of the sympathy something like that would gener-
ate, know what I mean?" he asked Josh with a wink.

"Yeah, I do," Josh answered, silently adding, *Unfortunately.* Maybe they should be looking at the manager,
too. The man certainly didn't seem upset by the mention of a murder, only that Green had kept it to himself.
Takes all kinds, he decided.

"So, what do you think?" Kennedy asked him the
moment they walked out of the small, crammed office.

"Compulsively cleaning his van every night before
bringing it in?" Josh repeated. "Hell, I think we just
found our suspect." He did a quick review of the facts in

his head. "Between this and that sketch, I think we've got enough to have the local ADA convince a judge to issue us a search warrant for the man's home and his so-called squeaky clean van."

"Aren't a couple of the Cavanaughs married to judges?" Kennedy asked him. "And the ADA," the older detective suddenly remembered, "she's a Cavanaugh, too, right? The chief of D's daughter, Janelle, as I recall."

Josh nodded. There was no denying it, the Cavanaughs were a very useful family to know.

"Does make things a little easier that way," he admitted. Personally, he couldn't understand why Bridget resisted the association for even a moment. If it had been him, he would have changed his return labels in a heartbeat. It was a win-win situation as far as he could see.

As he and Kennedy drew closer to where they'd left the car, Josh frowned. Quickening his pace, he hurried over to the backseat.

"Hey, where's the fire?" Kennedy called out, then protested, "I can't run, Youngblood. My knees gave out five years ago."

Coming to a stop beside Josh, Kennedy's attention was focused on him. He noted that Josh was scowling. "What's the matter?" Kennedy asked.

Josh gestured toward the backseat. "Notice anything missing?" he bit off, irritated.

The car was exactly where he'd left it. And it was empty, which was *not* exactly as he'd left it.

"Where's Bridget?" Kennedy asked.

"That's the question," Josh verified, fuming as he

looked around the immediate area. He didn't see her—
or anyone—around.

Kennedy was obviously not as disturbed about
Bridget's absence as he was. He shrugged his slightly
bowed shoulders and guessed, "Maybe she had to take
a break, you know, go looking for a ladies' room or
something."

But Josh was shaking his head as he scanned the
immediate area. "The woman's a camel. We were on a
stakeout once and I swear she didn't go once in twenty-
four hours, even though she had like four cups of
coffee." Josh looked around the backseat. There didn't
appear to have been a struggle. She'd left on her own,
he thought. Still, he had a bad, uneasy feeling about
this. "Where the hell did she get to?" he demanded.

"Why don't you call her on her cell and ask her?"
Kennedy suggested.

Annoyed that he hadn't thought of that himself, Josh
pressed the second programmed number on his keypad
and listened to the phone on the other end ring.

Once.

It went straight to voicemail.

"Damn it," he fumed. "When we find her and she's
all right, I'm going to kill her for taking off like that."

"That sounds reasonable," Kennedy quipped.

"'Reasonable' is wasted on that woman," Josh complained. "She thinks she's bulletproof."

"Okay, let's spread out and look for her," Kennedy
proposed. "She's on foot so she couldn't have gotten
very far."

"Yeah," Josh responded with absolutely no conviction in his voice.

The problem was, he thought, that Bridget might not be on foot.

The bad feeling in the pit of his stomach grew to almost unmanageable proportions.

Chapter 15

The same pain that had engulfed her as she was knocked out now yanked her back into consciousness.

The back of her skull throbbed. The pain was almost overwhelming and all but swallowed her up.

A moan rose in her throat, but something—instincts—kept her from allowing the sound to escape her lips.

It took only a few seconds for the fact that she was in motion to register.

Was she in Josh's car?

No, wait, there was something cold against her cheek. Metal, she was lying on some kind of metal floor. And she was being driven somewhere.

Very carefully she opened her eyelids just the tiniest bit, allowing only a hint of light in, not because her eyes were sensitive but because she didn't want anyone to see that she was coming to. *Someone* had hit her in the head and that same person had to be the one who was transporting her somewhere.

Where?

Opening her eyes a little more, Bridget saw that she was in the back of a van, lying facedown on the platform of a hydraulic lift ordinarily used to raise and lower wheelchair-bound travelers.

She realized that she was on the floor of the transport van at the same time that the fact that her wrists were bound with duct tape registered.

Doing her best to rise above the pain pounding along her aching skull, Bridget tried to remember what had happened.

Green.

She'd seen Green pulling up in the van in the rear of the lot. He was driving his transport van. When he got out, he'd started walking toward the main office. But before she could give Josh a heads-up, she saw Green suddenly do a U-turn on his heel. The next moment he was heading straight for his van again.

Apparently whatever he saw—Josh and Kennedy?—had spooked him.

There was no time to wonder what it was. If the transport driver took off, God knew when they'd be able to find him again.

So she'd gotten out of the backseat of the unmarked car and approached him.

"Excuse me," she'd called out just as he was about to get back into the van.

There was suspicion in his eyes when he looked in her direction. "Yeah?"

"My aunt's in a wheelchair and she's very fragile.

I can't get her in and out of my car anymore without risking having her fall. Problem is, she needs to go to a lot of doctors." She nodded toward his van. "Would you know what the company charges for a round trip?"

"Office handles that kind of stuff. You've gotta call them." He'd glanced around, then at her. "Where did you park?" he asked.

To avert any suspicion, she'd half turned to point toward a car across the street that she'd just noticed. That was when she felt as if her skull were being split open.

As the darkness claimed her, she thought that she was going to be the Lady Killer's final victim even though her hair wasn't red.

As she came to, she upbraided herself for turning her back, even slightly, on the man. Just because he was a serial killer didn't mean that he was stupid. Actually, the opposite was probably true. Planning had to go into remaining at large for three years and still carrying out his vendetta against any red-haired female who had the misfortune of crossing his path.

She was a blonde. Was she supposed to be his swan song? Or had he broadened his parameters? Why was she now lying on the floor of the van, her wrists bound? How had she tipped him off?

Her mouth wasn't taped shut. Why?

And then she had her answer. He wasn't growing sloppy, he just hadn't planned on another kill so soon. She saw an empty roll that had held duct tape discarded in the corner. He'd run out.

The van took a sharp turn to the right, then sped up. Glancing toward the door, she thought of the odds of pulling it open and jumping out before he saw she was awake and could stop her.

Not very good, she decided. Besides, they were going awfully fast and she could hear the sound of cars whizzing by.

Were they on the freeway? It sounded like it, but she wasn't sure. If they were, she wouldn't be able to jump clear of the van even if she did manage to open the door. Not with other cars moving so fast. She'd be run over.

Desperate to get her hands free, Bridget tried gnawing on the tape that bound her wrists. Several attempts got her nowhere. This would take too long, and who knew just how long she had?

Maybe she could pull him down from behind. Hoping that the music he was playing—music that made her head throb even more—would muffle any sound she made, Bridget began to inch her way over to him on the floor. She kept her eyes on the back of his head the entire time, praying he wouldn't turn around before she managed to reach him.

She crept toward him, frustrated by her maddeningly slow pace. If she moved faster, he might hear her.

As she debated how to pick her time and not get them both killed, she felt the van stopping. He was pulling up to a light.

They weren't on the freeway after all.

Now or never.

Pushing herself up to her knees, Bridget threw her bound arms forward around Green's throat and pulled back as hard as she could, trying to yank the man out of his seat.

Catching him off guard, Green had toppled backward against her. Horns from the cars around them began blasting, protesting the suddenly immobile van.

Green screamed a curse at her as she unseated him. "You bitch, you think this is going to save you? You're a dead woman, you hear me? A dead woman."

Because of the angle she'd used, Green had fallen on top of her, pinning her beneath him. She was still pulling against his throat as hard as she could, hoping to render him unconscious even after the air had whooshed out of her lungs.

She had to make him lose consciousness before he could do the same to her!

He was struggling, clawing at her, gasping for air.

And then she felt it. Felt something hard and sharp slash into her side. Felt something akin to fire burst out and engulfing her from the point of contact.

Suddenly, she wasn't able to hold on to him anymore, wasn't able to keep squeezing, robbing his lungs of his air supply. Her arms were just too weak. A darkness was returning for her.

He was free.

She could feel the driver's weight shifting, could feel his body separating from hers.

And then Bridget heard him yell, "Your heart is mine, bitch!"

Fear assaulted her. She was going to die.

As the thought registered in her dimming brain, something that sounded like a crack of thunder exploded inside the van.

Had they been hit by another car?

Had he killed her?

Sheets of flames were closing in around her. And

then, from somewhere in the distance, far, far away, she thought she heard Josh calling to her.

But that wasn't possible. Josh didn't know she was in here.

The next moment, the flames completely smothered her.

And then came oblivion.

"Call a bus, Kennedy. Damn it, call a bus!" Josh yelled, his voice cracking.

He was on his knees in the van, kneeling in Bridget's blood, wanting desperately to hold her to him, afraid to raise her from the floor. There was no longer any doubt that the man they had come after was the serial killer they'd been hunting. Less than a minute before he and Kennedy reached the van and threw the door open, the serial killer had viciously stabbed Bridget.

Josh had shouted out his warning at the same moment he'd discharged his weapon.

The threat was over.

Blood was now flowing from Bridget's side at a frightening rate. Fighting back his panic, Josh pressed the palms of his hands down hard against her side, trying to stop the blood from leaving her body.

Trying to keep her alive.

Terror kept surging through him. "You stay with me, Bridget, you hear me?" he demanded. "You stay with me! I won't let you die. You're not allowed to die. Damn you, anyway, why didn't you wait for us?"

Even in his addled state, Josh knew the answer to that. She hadn't waited because she probably saw the killer taking off. It wasn't in her nature to hang back and wait.

"Stay with me," he repeated, then pleaded again, "Stay with me."

"They're coming," Kennedy told him as he ended his call into the precinct.

She didn't have much time. He could see that. Even with his hands pressed against the wound, she was still losing blood.

"Tell them to come faster!" Josh roared. He tossed his head back, trying to get the tears in his eyes to clear. "I don't know how much longer she's going to be able to hang on."

"You kidding?" Kennedy countered, his own voice throbbing with emotion. Doing his best not to let his thoughts go toward a darker path. "This is Bridget. She's a fighter. She always has been. It'll take more than a stab wound to get her."

"Yeah," Josh agreed.

The word felt like dried straw inside his mouth.

They'd taken her from him.

He had refused to leave her side and had traveled inside the ambulance to the hospital, but once the paramedics reached the hospital, the emergency room surgeons came running out to the gurney and they had taken Bridget from him.

Leaving him to pace and haunt the corridor, feeling helpless and inadequate.

Leaving him to vacillate between beating himself up for keeping Bridget in the car when he knew what she was like and being furious with her for going after the killer herself.

And all the while, Josh kept staring at the operating

room doors, afraid to let himself think what was going on beyond the double doors.

Kennedy had followed the ambulance and arrived just behind it. After that, Josh had lost track of the older detective.

It didn't matter. Nothing mattered except Bridget living.

Leaning against the wall, Josh closed his eyes and prayed for a minute, vaguely remembering a fragment of a prayer from childhood.

He felt ancient.

And scared.

When Josh opened his eyes again a couple of minutes later, a tall, white-haired man with a kindly face was walking toward the O.R. The man was dressed all in black and he was wearing a clerical collar.

A priest.

No! Josh thought frantically. *No!*

As if to deny the man's very presence, to deny the *need* for the man's presence, Josh shifted, placing himself in front of the approaching priest.

As he stood there, a defiant human wall, Josh growled out, "She doesn't need a priest." But if someone inside the O.R. had sent for the man, if she was dying, then he had no right to deny this man access to Bridget.

He felt as if his heart was being ripped out of his chest.

"I'd like to think that everyone needs a priest once in a while," the man answered, his resonant voice sounding oddly comforting. "Bridget's father called me. I live less than a mile away from the hospital, so he knew I could get here before he did," the priest explained. He nodded toward the O.R. "Is Bridget in there?"

The priest's deep blue eyes were kind as they looked at him, Josh thought. He tried to make sense of what he was being told. If no one in the O.R. had called the man, then maybe she would be all right after all.

But then why was he here? And why would Bridget's father have called him?

Feeling lost and confused, it took Josh a moment to realize that the priest was extending his hand to him.

"I'm Bridget's Uncle Adam," he said, introducing himself.

Belatedly, Josh took the hand that was being offered and shook it. The words swam in his head. Her uncle? Oh, yeah, right. Bridget had an uncle who was part of the clergy. He knew that. Or had known that.

Right now, nothing was making sense in his head. All his thoughts were jumbled, as if a force field were keeping the absolutely unthinkable from finding him.

Seeing the confusion on the younger man's face, Adam said kindly, "I'm Sean's older brother. At least that was what we all thought before the hospital mix-up came to light," he said, amused. "For the record, I still consider myself Bridget's uncle. Takes more than blood to make family," he added with a wink.

Josh vaguely remembered saying the same thing to Bridget over an eternity ago, when he found her agonizing over her revised family tree. It felt odd hearing the sentiment echoed back to him.

Father Adam nodded toward the O.R. doors. "How is she doing?" he asked.

The helpless feeling was so oppressive, he was

having trouble breathing. Josh shook his head. "They won't tell me."

The priest took the non-information in stride. "I subscribe to the no-news-is-good-news school of thought," he said with a smile, and then he assured Josh, "Bridget's a fighter."

"So they tell me," Josh replied, hopelessness echoing in his voice.

"In her case, those are not just empty words," Father Adam said. "Let me tell you a little story, Detective. When Bridget was about ten years old, her family rented a cabin in the mountains one winter. She and her younger brother, Logan, snuck out one morning before anyone was up. They were expressly told not to go on the lake because the ice was thin that year." Father Adam's smile was a fond, indulgent one. "So naturally that was where Bridget and her brother went. Long story short, the ice broke right under Logan's feet when they were halfway across, plunging him into the icy lake. Bridget didn't panic, she didn't go running back to the cabin to get her father. She took off her coat, dove into the water and saved her brother. When she pulled him out, she wrapped him up in her coat and somehow managed to carry him back to the cabin. She literally saved his life.

"The downside of the story was Logan came down with the sniffles—and Bridget came down with a really bad case of pneumonia. So bad that she had to be hospitalized. Her parents were afraid that she was going die. Even the doctors were worried, telling them to prepare for the worst."

Listening, Josh nodded. "And she bounced back."

The priest smiled broadly. "That she did."

Josh blew out a breath. "Sounds like Bridget," he agreed, trying desperately to take heart from the story.

Bridget's uncle placed a large, ham-like hand comfortingly on his shoulder. "The point of the story is that Bridget always manages to come out on top no matter what the situation. Don't worry, boy. She's going to be all right."

God, but he wished he had the priest's conviction, Josh thought.

Before he could say anything in response, Josh heard a commotion down the hall. It grew louder. Curious, he took a few steps toward the growing din, thinking to investigate. Looking for a distraction.

The distraction came to him.

The commotion came from what amounted to an army of people. It was headed by the chief of detectives who was walking beside Bridget's father, Sean. Behind them was what appeared to be half the police department. Or, at the very least, half the people who had been at the party the other night to officially welcome Bridget's grandfather.

As they drew closer, the approaching Cavanaughs managed to fill every single space in the corridor, and while the noise they made couldn't exactly be referred to as deafening, it was definitely noticeable.

A couple of moments later, a weary-looking nurse approached the group from another direction. She stopped right beside Josh. It was obvious from the expression on the older woman's face that she recognized at least a large number of the people who now stood in the corridor, shifting back and forth as they made an attempt not to block it.

Sighing, the senior nurse said to no one in particular,

"I knew this was going to happen the minute I saw that last name on the insurance form. You know, between getting shot and giving birth, you Cavanaughs should seriously think about getting your own hospital annex," she said, this time addressing her comment to Brian.

"You make sure our Bridget makes it," Andrew answered, speaking up from the rear, "and we'll see about making that happen."

"Don't toy with me, Andrew Cavanaugh," the nurse fired back, pretending to complain. "I'm a very vulnerable woman."

Andrew laughed at her comment. "I'm counting on that, Virginia."

Even as he answered her, more and more family members arrived, alerted by the others.

Greetings as well as repeated questions filled the air.

The head nurse pointed toward the recently remodeled and greatly expanded waiting room. The facility bore more of a resemblance to an arena than a room.

"The hospital would appreciate at least *some* of you waiting in there." Her features pulled into a faux scowl. "No one can get by with all of you clogging the hallway like this."

"And if we go in there to wait the way you want," Brian bargained, "in exchange, you'll come by and give us regular updates on how my niece is doing?"

"Yes, yes, anything to get you people out of the hallway," Virginia promised.

As she gestured again toward the waiting room, the members of the family slowly began to file by her, taking seats or opting to stand as they all gave one another comfort.

The nurse looked at Josh expectantly. "You, too, young man," she urged.

"He's only one person," Father Adam pointed out. "And her partner. If there's an ounce of mercy in you, I'd let him stay exactly where he is," he advised gently.

After a momentary debate, Virginia begrudgingly nodded. "All right, you can stay," she told Josh, then turned to look at all the others. "But as for the rest of you—"

She didn't need to finish her sentence.

Dutifully, the family members who hadn't retreated into the room yet did so now.

"I am holding you to your promise," Andrew said to the nurse as he followed the last of the combined family into the waiting area.

The nurse nodded. "And I'll keep it," Virginia told him solemnly. Glancing again at the young man leaning against the wall beside the O.R. doors, she withdrew for now. But she would be back and soon, just as she'd promised. Virginia Gibbs knew better than to ignore the former chief of police.

Chapter 16

Seven heavy layers were pressing down on her. Smothering her. Seven layers of hot, searing pain, determined to keep her submerged in a hazy, oppressive, formless world.

Bridget struggled, desperately trying to surface.

Her eyelids felt as if they each weighed a ton apiece. Maybe more. They refused to open.

She refused to give up.

Eventually, an eternity later, she won.

But when she finally opened her eyes, she didn't recognize her surroundings. Only that she'd never been here before.

This wasn't her bed, or her room. And who was that with his head down on the bland blanket that covered the bed and her?

Slowly, the answers came into focus.

This was a hospital room. And her side hurt like hell. Moreover, something must have clearly crawled into her mouth and died there because not only was there a terrible taste inside her mouth, but her lips felt as if they'd been glued together. It hurt to pull them apart.

She did it anyway.

Trying to speak, Bridget wound up moaning instead. Her eyes closed again.

Josh jerked his head up, alert the second he heard the sound. His neck protested the sudden motion, aching because of the position he'd unintentionally assumed when he'd finally fallen asleep. He'd been at her bedside for over two days now, keeping vigil over her. Waiting for Bridget to open her eyes and finally wake up.

"Bridget?" He whispered her name hesitantly, afraid he'd only *thought* he'd heard her. Or maybe he'd only dreamed it and his desire to make it true had propelled him into an awakened state.

Bridget dragged in a ragged breath. "Uh-huh," she managed to push out. With supreme effort, she opened her eyes again.

He'd never seen anything half as beautiful as those blue eyes of hers.

"Oh thank God," Josh cried, grasping her hand in both of his. "I was starting to think that you weren't ever going to open your eyes."

It was still a struggle to keep her eyelids up. And then, it was as if someone had opened a giant door in a cloud. Her memory of the last few minutes that she'd been conscious came flooding back to her. Surrounding her. Josh had found her. Rescued her.

Josh.

"How did you…"

Her energy ebbed away from her before she could finish the question. She tried again, determined to be heard. When she spoke, her voice was a little bit stronger. She peeled each word away from the roof of her mouth.

"How did you find me?"

Josh laughed shortly. As if he would have ever given up looking until he found her.

"Easy," he quipped. "I just asked around for the biggest pain in the butt in the area. It was never any contest," he told her, wanting to take her in his arms and just hold her.

But Bridget was in pain, despite the medication. He could see that and he knew if he followed through on his impulse, he would only be hurting her.

"No, seriously," she pressed hoarsely. "How did you find me?" She had to know why she was so lucky when others hadn't been. How he had tracked her when so many other women before her had fallen victim to the Lady Killer's knife.

"Your earbud," he told her. It was a miracle that it hadn't gotten dislodged and fallen out when she'd been kidnapped. He wasn't about to think what might have happened if she'd lost that tiny piece of electronic equipment.

Bridget blinked, confused. "What?"

"That transmitter you still had in your ear, it was on. I called in and had the lab tech locate the frequency in order to track it. That's how I found you."

He remembered that horrid pain in the pit of his gut when he'd realized that she must have been taken by their suspect. But it was nothing in comparison to the way he had felt when the van had abruptly stopped moving.

Praying she wasn't dead, he'd run, his weapon drawn, to intercept the van. He'd torn opened the back door and had been just in time to keep her from receiving a fatal stab wound from the driver's drawn knife. That was when he'd seen that there was already blood on it. And that there was blood all around Bridget's prone body on the floor.

"Oh," she managed to murmur, then said, "I dreamed you were yelling at me." Each word was a little easier to utter than the last, but her mouth still felt as if she'd had sand for lunch. Sand that had trickled down her throat.

"That wasn't a dream," he told her simply. "I did."

Her eyes drew together. "You yelled at me? But I was just stabbed," she protested.

"And you were also an idiot," he countered, anger suddenly surging through him when he thought of how close he had come to losing her. "*That* was why I was yelling at you."

His tone was accusatory, masking the raw, vulnerable emotion just beneath. If something had happened to her, he wouldn't have ever been able to live with himself.

"Who the hell told you to get into that van and try to take Green down single-handedly?" Josh angrily demanded.

"I didn't get into the van," she protested.

"Then how—"

Bridget wet her lips. They were sticking together again.

"He must have knocked me out and dragged me into

the van." She blinked, trying to remember the order in which everything had to have happened. "I saw him drive up while you and Kennedy were inside the office, taking to the manager. Green must have seen something that tipped him off. I saw him hurrying back to the van. I got out to talk to him. I knew I had to stall him until you came. Otherwise, he could just vanish on us again."

Touching the back of her head, Bridget winced. The pain from that area was unexpected. "He must've hit me when I turned my head to look at something." She closed her eyes for a moment, trying to distance herself from what she remembered. "When I came to, my wrists were duct taped together and I was in the back of the van, on the floor. I knew if I didn't do something, he was going to kill me." As she took another ragged breath, her lungs ached in protest. She would feel like hell for a while, Bridget thought, resigning herself to the fact. "How long have I been out?"

"Three days," he told her.

She'd expected to hear that she'd been unconscious for a few hours, not days. The latter was scary. And then something else occurred to her. She looked at him. The man definitely appeared worn out. "And you've been here the whole time?" she asked in disbelief.

Josh shrugged, trying to make light of it. "Didn't seem to be much of a point to be anywhere else." Because that focused too closely on his own vulnerable state, he changed the subject. "A lot of your family's been by. New and old," he added. "When they heard you'd been hurt, they almost took over the whole damn hospital. They're an impressive group of people," he admitted. He saw a weak smile curving her mouth and found it immensely heartening. "Oh, by the way, I finally got to meet your Uncle Adam. He's a really nice guy. How come you never brought him around?" he asked.

She was going to shrug, but that, it turned out, hurt too so she stopped midmotion. "It never occurred to me. Why? Did you want to make a confession?"

He was still holding her hand, he realized. But he didn't let go. His eyes met hers. "Not to him."

Her sense of protectiveness rose to the fore. "What's wrong with my uncle?"

"Nothing," he answered simply. "But if I was going to confess something, it would be to—" And then he shrugged again. He wanted to pick his time, and this wasn't it. "Never mind."

Pressing the control button beside her, Bridget managed to elevate the back of her bed so that she was in more of a sitting position. "You know I hate it when you do that, start saying something and don't finish it."

Well, if they were going to compare dislikes, his trumped hers, he thought. "And I hate you acting like some superheroine who thinks she's bulletproof."

Where did he get off taking her to task for anything? "You've got a lousy bedside manner, Youngblood, you know that?"

Sometimes she could get him so mad, he could shake her. Did she know what she meant to him? That she was more than just his partner, although that was a pretty big deal in itself. And did she even realize that what she'd done could have cost her her life?

"Maybe that's because I don't want to be standing at a hospital bedside." His expression softened. "I'd rather be standing next to the bed in your apartment—as long as you were in it."

She opened her mouth twice, but retorts didn't come. A third attempt had her saying, "Okay, fair enough." She looked around on either side of her on the bed. "Where's the call button?"

"Why do you want the call button for?" He was on his feet beside her. "Do you need the doctor? Are you in pain?"

"To get the nurse. Not necessarily. And yeah, pretty much," she said, answering all three of his questions in order.

His suspicions raised, Josh eyed her closely as he asked, "Why do you want the nurse?"

Her mouth curved. "To help me get dressed and out of here so I can get back to my apartment and have you stand next to my bed," she told him, her eyes saying a good deal more. "Weren't you paying attention to what you just said?"

Much as he wanted her to himself right now, her place was here until the doctors thought she was strong enough to go home. "You're not going anywhere," he informed her sternly.

Bridget raised her chin, ready for a fight. "You can't boss me around."

"I saved your life," he pointed out. "Technically, it now belongs to me, so yeah, I can boss you around if I want to."

She eyed him for a moment and just when he thought she was going to put up a fight, she quietly asked, "And what do you plan on doing with this extra life you've got on your hands?"

He said the first thing that popped into his head. "What I'd like to do is shove it into a closet to keep it safe."

She laughed softly, relaxing. Suddenly very glad to be alive. And that he had been there to save her. "There are laws against that, you know."

"Yeah, I know. I guess the only other way to keep watch over you and make sure you don't do something else to get yourself killed is to marry you."

After what had just happened in the last few days, she would have thought that she was prepared for anything. Apparently, she wasn't.

Her mouth dropped open and she stared at Josh for a long moment before finally deciding that she was hallucinating again. She had to be. There was no way her carefree, footloose partner had just voluntarily offered to give up his no-strings-attached bachelorhood by proposing to her.

With that thought racing through her head, she felt her eyelids getting heavy again. Before she knew it, she'd nodded off.

"Talk about being cool," Josh murmured, adjusting her blanket. "She falls asleep in the middle of my marriage proposal."

When she opened her eyes again, there was no light shining in through the hospital window.

It was nighttime, she realized.

Her eyelids didn't feel heavy this time, but her eyes did feel gritty. And then, as before, she saw that she wasn't alone.

Seeing him made her smile from the inside out.

"You're still here," she said to Josh in a voice that sounded both surprised and pleased.

Sitting beside her bed, he brightened. He would never tire of seeing her open her eyes, Josh thought.

Each time he saw her do it, it felt like he was experiencing a minor miracle after that awful scare he'd endured.

"Still waiting for an answer," he told her mildly.

She tried to center her thoughts. "What was the question again?"

He phrased it formally now. If there had been any jitters associated with this, they had long since left him. "Bridget Cavelli-Cavanaugh, will you marry me?"

She drew out the moment before answering him. "Aren't you supposed to say something like, 'I love you,' before you ask something like that?"

She was stalling. Why? "You already know I love you."

"No, I don't," she protested. "I'm not a mind reader."

He grinned wickedly. Bridget was back, he thought, loving every second of this. "That wasn't my mind you were staring at the other night."

"Don't try to distract me." She took another deep breath. Mercifully, this one hurt a little less. "I'm waiting."

"I love you," he told her very seriously, then impishly grinned as he asked, "Now will you say yes?"

"You really want to do this?" she asked incredulously. Part of her still believed that there was a punch line somewhere in the offing.

"Yeah," he told her, gently brushing her hair away from her face. "I really want to do this. I know I can't talk you into playing it a little safer and not charging in without thinking it through, but I at least want to be able to fill every moment of my life with you whenever I can for as long as I can."

"Then I better not say no," she concluded.

This had gone easier than he'd anticipated. Bridget could be very perverse at times. "If you do, I'll just have to keep asking you until you finally break down and say yes."

"Then this'll save us both a lot of time," she concluded, tongue in check.

"Saving time. I'm all for that," he agreed

Her eyes told him just how much she loved him. "As long as you're for me, nothing else matters," she whispered.

"Always," he promised.

Bridget cocked her head slightly as she regarded him. "Are you going to keep talking, or are you going to kiss me?"

Josh didn't answer, at least not verbally. Lovingly framing her face with his hands, he went with door number two.

* * * * *

SUSPENSE

COMING NEXT MONTH
AVAILABLE APRIL 24, 2012

REQUEST YOUR FREE BOOKS!
2 FREE NOVELS PLUS 2 FREE GIFTS!

 Harlequin®

ROMANTIC
SUSPENSE

Sparked by Danger, Fueled by Passion.

YES! Please send me 2 FREE Harlequin® Romantic Suspense novels and my 2 FREE gifts (gifts are worth about $10). After receiving them, if I don't wish to receive any more books, I can return the shipping statement marked "cancel." If I don't cancel, I will receive 4 brand-new novels every month and be billed just $4.49 per book in the U.S. or $5.24 per book in Canada. That's a saving of at least 14% off the cover price! It's quite a bargain! Shipping and handling is just 50¢ per book in the U.S. and 75¢ per book in Canada.* I understand that accepting the 2 free books and gifts places me under no obligation to buy anything. I can always return a shipment and cancel at any time. Even if I never buy another book, the two free books and gifts are mine to keep forever.

240/340 HDN FEFR

Name _____ (PLEASE PRINT)

Address _____ Apt. #

City _____ State/Prov. _____ Zip/Postal Code

Signature (if under 18, a parent or guardian must sign)

Mail to the **Reader Service:**
IN U.S.A.: P.O. Box 1867, Buffalo, NY 14240-1867
IN CANADA: P.O. Box 609, Fort Erie, Ontario L2A 5X3

Not valid for current subscribers to Harlequin Romantic Suspense books.

Want to try two free books from another line?
Call 1-800-873-8635 or visit www.ReaderService.com.

* Terms and prices subject to change without notice. Prices do not include applicable taxes. Sales tax applicable in N.Y. Canadian residents will be charged applicable taxes. Offer not valid in Quebec. This offer is limited to one order per household. All orders subject to credit approval. Credit or debit balances in a customer's account(s) may be offset by any other outstanding balance owed by or to the customer. Please allow 4 to 6 weeks for delivery. Offer available while quantities last.

Your Privacy—The Reader Service is committed to protecting your privacy. Our Privacy Policy is available online at www.ReaderService.com or upon request from the Reader Service.

We make a portion of our mailing list available to reputable third parties that offer products we believe may interest you. If you prefer that we not exchange your name with third parties, or if you wish to clarify or modify your communication preferences, please visit us at www.ReaderService.com/consumerschoice or write to us at Reader Service Preference Service, P.O. Box 9062, Buffalo, NY 14269. Include your complete name and address.

HRS11B

*Colby Investigator Lyle McCaleb is on the case.
But can he protect Sadie Gilmore from her haunting past?*

**Harlequin Intrigue® presents a new installment
in Debra Webb's miniseries, COLBY, TX.**

Enjoy a sneak peek of COLBY LAW.

With the shotgun hanging at her side, she made it as far as the porch steps, when the driver's side door opened. Sadie knew the deputies in Coryell County. Her visitor wasn't any of them. A boot hit the ground, stirring the dust. Something deep inside her braced for a new kind of trouble. As the driver emerged, Sadie's gaze moved upward, over the gleaming black door and the tinted window to a black Stetson and dark sunglasses. She couldn't quite make out the details of the man's face but some extra sense that had nothing to do with what she could see set her on edge.

Another boot hit the ground and the door closed. Her visual inspection swept over long legs cinched in comfortably worn denim, a lean waist and broad shoulders testing the seams of a shirt that hadn't come off the rack at any store where she shopped, finally zeroing in on the man's face just as he removed the dark glasses.

The weapon almost slipped from her grasp. Her heart bucked hard twice, then skidded to a near halt.

Lyle McCaleb.

"What the...devil?" whispered past her lips.

Unable to move a muscle, she watched in morbid fascination as he hooked the sunglasses on to his hip pocket and strode toward the house—toward her. Sadie wouldn't have been able to summon a warning that he was trespassing had her life depended on it.

Lyle glanced at the shotgun as he reached up and removed his hat. "Expecting company?"

As if her heart had suddenly started to pump once more, kicking her brain into gear, fury blasted through her frozen muscles. "What do you want, Lyle McCaleb?"

"Seeing as you didn't know I was coming, that couldn't be for me." He gave a nod toward her shotgun.

This could not be happening. Seven years he'd been gone. This was…this was… "I have nothing to say to you." She turned her back to him and walked away. Who did she think he was, showing up here like this after all this time? It was crazy. He was crazy!

"I know I'm the last person on this earth you want to see."

Her feet stopped when she wanted to keep going. To get inside the house and slam the door and dead bolt it.

"We need to talk."

The stakes are high as Lyle fights for the woman he loves. But can he solve the case in time to save an innocent life?

Find out in COLBY LAW
Available May 2012 from Harlequin Intrigue®
wherever books are sold.

The heartwarming conclusion of

from fan-favorite author
TINA LEONARD

With five brothers married, Jonas Callahan is under no
pressure to tie the knot. But when Sabrina McKinley
admits her bouncing baby boy is his, Jonas does
everything he can to win over the woman he's loved
for years. First the last Callahan bachelor must uncover
an important family secret…before he can take
the lovely Sabrina down the aisle!

A Callahan Wedding

**Available this May
wherever books are sold.**

Harlequin *Presents*®

Royalty has never been so scandalous!

THE
SANTINA
CROWN

When Crown Prince Alessandro of Santina proposes
to paparazzi favorite Allegra Jackson it promises
to be *the* social event of the decade!

Harlequin Presents® invites you to step into the decadent
playground of the world's rich and famous and rub shoulders
with royalty, sheikhs and glamorous socialites.

**Collect all 8 passionate tales written by *USA TODAY*
bestselling authors, beginning May 2012!**